REDEEMING LUCIFER

REDEEMING LUCIFER

A spiritual adventure

Lennart Svensson

A record of this publication is available from the British Library.

ISBN 978-1-910027-20-2

Typesetting by Wordzworth Ltd
www.wordzworth.com

Cover design by Titanium Design Ltd
www.titaniumdesign.co.uk

Printed by Lightning Source UK
www.lightningsource.com

Cover image: The Battle of Alexander at Issus
by Albrecht Altdorfer (Alamy Photostock)

Published by Local Legend
www.local-legend.co.uk

LOCAL
LEGEND

About this Book

Carl Griffensteen is a captain in the Russian army at the time of the Romanian campaign of 1917. Given the mission to reconnoitre quarters for the regimental staff at a nearby castle, he arrives with his trusted striker Ivan to be invited in for dinner by the enigmatic lord of the castle, Count Alexandru. But from this moment, Carl's life takes a most unexpected turn and nothing will ever again be quite what it seems…

This extraordinary writing is a page-turning spiritual adventure story that finds our heroes journeying through parallel, mystical worlds where the creatures and landscapes mirror the archetypes and emotions of their inner minds. Their epic quest is no less than to find and offer redemption to Lucifer himself, thereby healing the world of its ills. Naturally, there are some very powerful forces that want them to fail.

Many challenges are overcome, some more by good fortune than judgement, until Carl and his allies must fight the cosmically decisive Battle of Gnipaheden, the ultimate struggle between good and evil.

Redeeming Lucifer is a tale in the finest tradition of legendary deeds, a wonderful blend of esotericism, pure imagination and acutely observed historical fact. It is also one that challenges us all to examine the deeper purposes of our own lives.

The Author

Lennart Svensson is a Swedish academic living in Härnösand on the northern Swedish coast. He grew up in a virtual wilderness of wooded hills and farmland, listening to his grandmother telling fairy-tales of old. Later, he cherished the stories of modern fantasy writers. Thus was born *Redeeming Lucifer*, his debut novel in English.

He has a BA in Indology, and enjoys cooking and reading classics.

Previous Publications

Lennart has published prose works in Swedish, notably his first novel, *Antropolis* (Etherion Forlag, 2009), a spiritual vision of the future, while in English he has published *Borderline – A Traditionalist Outlook for Modern Man* (Numen Books, 2015), a clarion call for idealism in this modern age of materialism. His first ever fiction in English was the story *The Middle Zone*, published in *Morpheus Tales: The Best Weird Fiction, Volume 3* (2013).

Since 2007 Lennart has been blogging at *The Svensson Galaxy*.

Contents

CHAPTER ONE

THE MISSION

The colonel was looking at the map, laid out on the table. His finger was moving over the sheet, circling around an area and finally pointing at it. "Here, my friends! We're going here. We have to take up defensive positions at the Dirava river."

The operations officer, a lieutenant colonel standing beside him at the table, nodded and said, "That sounds feasible. It is the only way to stop the German advance."

"Hmm," mused the chief quartermaster, a bespectacled major, "then we'll have to reconnoitre for a new HQ, I figure?"

"What would you suggest?" asked the colonel. The major, looking through his round glasses as he scrutinised the map, caught sight of a village.

"Here's a village… and here's a castle. Castle Munte, it says. That should be excellent."

"I guess we'll have to send out a man to check it out," the major said. "Sergeant!"

A NCO rose from his desk and approached. The major told him to fetch Captain Griffensteen. "Tell him he's going for a ride." The sergeant saluted, turned and left the room. Passing along a corridor and turning a corner, he eventually reached the furthest door where he stopped and knocked.

"Enter!" was heard from the other side. The sergeant entered a room that had a desk full of papers, a window overlooking a mauve-tinted autumn day, a chair over which a grey army tunic hung and a shelf on which a service cap lay; on another chair hung a scabbard and a revolver belt, whilst a pair of riding boots stood on the floor. Finally there was a bed in which an elegant, brooding officer lay. The man had brownish hair, a narrow face with some-what protruding cheekbones and grey eyes, the eyes of a dreamer. He was clad in a grey cotton shirt and grey-blue breeches with red stripes. For the moment he lay reading the Bible.

The sergeant saluted. "Captain, Sergeant Kusovsky reporting for duty. Your presence is needed in the Staff Room. You're going for a ride, they say."

"Understood, Sergeant," the captain said. "Dismissed."

The captain laid his Bible aside. He was an officer of the Russian army and a Finnish Swede, a *finlandssvensk* as the native term has it, an ethnically Swedish Finlander yet a subject of the Russian crown like all Finlanders. He reached for his boots and put them on. He really liked these boots, smooth and tough at the same time, comfortable to wear and enduring every weather. The Russians sure knew how to make boots, he thought, having worn them in battle since 1914. Then he stood up and donned his tunic, made of tightly woven wool, called cloth. Finally he girded his loins with a belt and headed for the Staff Room. Once there he reported for duty to the bespectacled major.

The major for his part smiled, saying, "You're going out for a ride, mate! You're going to reconnoitre staff cantonments in a castle, Castle Munte, some ten kilometres from here. The staff to be quartered will be thirty men plus supply vans, all with stables for fifty horses, so this castle could do. It's your job to see if it does. And if it does, then you have carte blanche to negotiate a contract. You know the drill."

"Yes, Major."

"You can take one striker with you. Or don't. You choose. As long as you're back within twenty-four hours."

"Will do, Major!"

Carl went to the field map on the table, studying the 1:50000 scale topography, noting where he was going and drawing a sketch to aid his memory. Then he ordered the sergeant to equip two horses with provisions for two men.

Having received his orders in writing, Carl left the room and returned to his own. Sitting on the bed, he checked that his Nagant revolver was loaded then got up and donned revolver belt and sword-belt with scabbard. 'Hot lead and cold steel', he thought, 'now I'm prepared for everything!' Picking up some spare clothes he put them in a bag along with weapon accessories and a tooth-brush, a pipe and tobacco. Whistling, he put on topcoat and service cap, took his gloves and bag and left the room, taking the stairs down and venturing out into the yard.

There, a groom already stood waiting with two horses, a black one with white blaze and a brown one with black mane and tail. Carl approached the saddle bag of the black horse, opened it and put his bag in it. The other saddle bag was full with provisions like preserves, a piece of bread and some smoked ham. 'Such an adventure,' Carl thought, 'this is better than sitting around at the HQ, drawing maps and writing reports.'

He had no idea just what an adventure this would turn out to be.

Carl told the groom to wait while he himself picked out a fol-lower for this trip since he had, indeed, decided to have a striker along. An aide to the regimental aide, he thought that sounded appropriate. Going into a nearby house with quarters for the striker squad, he had the men lined up and chose a shortish, crew-cut, moon-faced fellow with a glint in his pale blue eyes. He just looked right. Ivan Ivanovich Masov was the man's name.

Five minutes later the pair, Carl and Ivan, rode out from the HQ yard under a brooding grey sky. The temperature was 15 degrees on this September's day in 1917, September the 7th as it happened. It was one o'clock in the afternoon. While riding along a sandy street lined with small shacks, finely built wooden houses and the odd stone house, Carl told Ivan about their mission to recce for staff cantonments in a castle some ten kilometres away. The two riders passed a field replete with tents, men and horses. Next, having crossed a deserted lot, they reached a westward road leading to the Transylvanian mountains, which could be seen in the distance. And thus he was off on his adventure, the grey-clad Carl Griffensteen, later to be known as the Grey Knight, off to the mountains, to a far land and beyond, off to fight the greatest battle on Earth to redeem evil – and then some.

He knew nothing about this greater mission now. But as things stood and being the man he was, he was indeed prepared for everything.

As they trotted over a field, Carl asked Ivan, "Experienced rider?"

"Yes, sir," Ivan said. "Joining the cavalry was like coming home. I hadn't even seen a horse before the war but as soon as I could mount one it all seemed natural."

Carl nodded. It made sense, the man seemed to know what he was doing. "And now we're heading out in the field," he continued, "out on a little mission, by the grace of God. Better than to play 17-4 all day long, eh?"

Ivan smiled for an answer, it being appropriate for this kind of small talk. They left the field and entered a deciduous woodland, the trees still retaining their green leaves. For a moment the sun shone through a rip in the clouds, making the glade bathe in a golden-green hue. They passed over a brock by a stone bridge. Ahead, the country became more hilly, the birch accompanied by pine and spruce.

"Do you believe in God?" Carl asked his aide incidentally.

"Yes, yes I do."

"So do you have Him with you now?"

Ivan smiled. "I don't exactly know about that. But I know that He's there somewhere."

Carl contented himself with that answer. As for himself, he recognised God within himself. "Ye are gods," as Jesus had said. "The kingdom of God is within you," he'd also said. You had to realise your inner divinity, the light within; this was Carl's creed. To be an esotericist of this kind, to be literally oriented towards the inner self, that wasn't so common these days but Carl was no common man. True, he was no saint. However, he had the feeling that experiencing the God nature, the divine light within, was the starting point for everything – morality, politics, art... everything!

Inspired by the Gospel of John, Carl's mantra was the 'I Am'. This was the formula for being a man, a sentient, spiritually minded man, the I Am saying symbolising the esoteric concept of divinity that Carl cherished. The source of the I Am formula was Christ saying things such as, "I am the light of the world... I am the good shepherd... I am the way, the truth and the life... I am the true vine..." and so on.

They rode through a mountainous woodland with watching yellow wolves' eyes and hooting owls. The sky was once again overcast, the sun having decided to stay above the cloud layer for the remainder of the day, and soon they ventured into the Transylvanian hills.

As a Finnish Swede, the venerable Carl Griffensteen had been born on the barony family estate outside the Finnish coastal town of Vasa, in 1893. He was the youngest of five siblings, three sisters and one brother besides himself. His brother Axel became head of the family when their father died in 1907, this prompting Carl to settle for a military career. With the help of some friends in high places, he moved to Russia in 1909, entering the military academy in Moscow and from 1912 serving in a provincial regiment in Belarus.

From a career point of view, he welcomed the outbreak of the First World War, being something to break the stalemate. And after some weeks serving as an HQ orderly officer, he was given command of a platoon of the 77th Jekaterinski Hussars. The death toll had been large after Tannenberg and the Masurian Lakes and vacancies were plentiful. He led his cavalry troop, as the mounted infantry it was transformed into, in the new era of machine gun fire and was promoted to first lieutenant. In 1916, he was further promoted to captain and led a cavalry company during the stalemate after the Brusilov offensive. Then, in the spring of 1917, he received the assignment as regimental aide, duly showing up at the 34th Ivanovski Cavalry Regiment in Ternopol and quickly instructed into this new job as a glorified assistant for the regimental commander.

By this time there was a tug-of-war over Romania. Romania eventually chose the Russian camp. But the Germans still wanted to lay their hands on her, resulting in many land battles between German and Russian forces from 1916 onwards. Then, in September 1917, the operations focused on the river Dirava and thus Carl got the task of riding in advance to a castle where the regimental HQ would be accommodated.

Carl and Ivan now passed through a deserted land, a country ravaged by fire, its fields and pastures black with soot and its houses smoky ruins. Among the remains of a house, among charred beams and the naked chimney stack pointing to the sky in an accusing gesture, Carl saw a skinny dog trotting about. Near a burned-down barn, dead bodies were seen, the sickly sweet smell of putrefaction being carried along by the wind. Had they been shot by raiding Germans? Or by robber bands, free to act when the sociopolitical fabric had been ripped asunder by the war?

Carl couldn't know but it annoyed him. This wasn't the war he had ventured out into three years ago. Being a second lieutenant in a White Russian country regiment at the time of mobilisation, he wanted to fight pitched battles against the Germans, not to chase bandits or clean up among death and destruction. But this was also part of it, he had learned. In 1914 he'd known nothing about gas, ten-hour long barrages and rides through deserted, ravaged lands, but now he knew them by heart. As a youngster he had dreamed of outings in fairy lands, of adventures where everything was clear-cut and heroic. In the real world, nothing was so heroic but he wanted it to be. Wasn't there an unambiguous adventure to be experienced somewhere? Wasn't there, somewhere, a land of dreams where you knew there were impossible things to do and experience? A land of castles on the misty horizon, of flying cities in the air, of fair maidens in lush gardens inviting you to wine and dine? A land of pulsating life and meaningfulness, an alternative to this world where the nihilists and the pessimists and the ironists always seemed to get the upper hand, the final say? This he asked himself, this was Carl the dreamer, the stern officer and war hero with the eyes of a dreamer.

They were scouting the countryside for a staff cantonment, their orders expressly being to visit Castle Munte and investigate it. According to Carl's sketch, a village lay at the foothills of the castle proper. And in the afternoon they reached the village, called Merlinatu.

Riding into the village they soon encountered a church. Sitting at the junction of three roads, a fork, the sight of it made Carl say thanks to the Lord. He simply liked the look of the place, an eastern Catholic church of mixed Romano-Russian features such as gilded onion domes on the twin towers, a white-washed façade and round arches above the entry and the windows.

They rode up to the church, dismounted and bound their steeds to a gate through which they entered and approached the front door. True to their nature as men of war, they remained armed but took off their headgear, entering the main hall with its lighted candles, walls covered by rich hangings and an altar with a large cross of gold, decorated with rubies and emeralds. Ivan took himself off to a side chapel where he lit a candle. Carl for his part sat down on a pew and admired the vaults above him, the textile art and a backdrop painting of Mary and the infant Jesus. The burning incense enchanted him and made him dreamy; closing his eyes, he meditated on the mantra 'I Am'. He needed this kind of meditation in face of the daunting task ahead, a task he only vaguely discerned.

Awakening from his reveries finally, Carl found himself looking up into the mild eyes of the Virgin Mary. 'Bless you', he thought.

The captain rose and headed for the door, followed by Ivan. Out in the street, Carl asked a passing farmer for the way to the castle and they mounted their horses, leaving the village and following a road leading up into the mountains. It got darker. A full moon rose and illuminated the woods and the rocks. Eventually, in the distance, a castle was seen with high walls, steep roofs and a drawbridge. It was their goal, Castle Munte.

Carl and Ivan rode over the bridge and entered the courtyard, left the horses to a servant and were shown into the building proper. There another servant took their caps and coats. Finally, standing in a resplendent hall, they were met by an elegant, pale man with well-groomed, dark hair and a rose in the button-hole of his dinner jacket.

"Welcome, Captain Griffensteen," the man said.

"Thank you," Carl said. "How do you know my name?"

"I know this and that. I also know that your servant's name is Ivan Ivanovich. And I am Count Alexandru, at your service." The man bowed and smiled a disconcerting, cold smile. Carl shuddered inwardly but kept his poise, shaking hands with the man.

CHAPTER TWO
CASTLE MUNTE

The hall was decorated with portraits on the walls depicting lordly men in a variety of elaborate headgear, fur coats and embroidered tunics. Carl nodded towards them, said something polite about the interior decor and then got down to the business of cantoning the staff.

"Indeed, that's your errand?" the Count asked. "I would love to quarter your regimental staff. However, I have already been asked this question, by a German."

"A German?" Carl raised his eyebrows in surprise.

"Indeed. A German unit also wants the castle for their quarters. As for their officer, he's here right now. In fact, we're about to have dinner. Would you like to join us at our table and discuss the matter there?"

Carl accepted the invitation on the spot. Ivan, for his part, was invited to eat in the kitchen, which the striker seemed to relish. He was led off to the back rooms while Carl was given a room in which to refresh himself.

A while later Carl entered the banquet hall, clad in his boots and breeches and officer's tunic and a clean shirt to go with it. The hall for its part had visible, tarred rafters of oak in the roof, silk carpets, illuminated sconces and walls decorated with shields, spears and escutcheons. In a far corner one could also see some hunting trophies, wooden mounts with the heads of boar, deer and wolf, their jaws opened in eternal, threatening cries. The place had a certain barbaric splendour, Carl thought.

The main attraction of the room was the long dinner table, set with silver plates, goblets and cutlery on a dark green tablecloth. Two guests were already seated, a man and a woman. The woman was a dark beauty with hair fixed in an elaborate bun; she wore a golden necklace and a shimmering dress in red, purple and violet. She winked invitingly at Carl and he nodded slightly in return, approaching her.

Standing at the head of the table, Count Alexandru introduced them.

"Madame Parysatis, Captain Griffensteen."

"I am honoured," Carl said, taking the lady's hand and kissing it.

"So you just decided to drop by?" she asked.

"More or less," Carl said, stating his mission to reconnoitre for his staff.

"What a coincidence," the lady said, "because that is exactly what Colonel Körner is also here for!"

"Indeed, so I have just heard," Carl said and went over to the other side of the table to introduce himself to the other dinner guest. The German had already risen and now greeted Carl with an outstretched hand.

"Lieutenant Colonel Körner, at your service," the man said, looking at Carl through his monocle. He had a stern, straight face, what some would call 'a nutcracker's face', with a high forehead, a crewcut and blue, intelligent eyes.

"I seem to be standing before the face of my enemy," Carl said casually, recognising the insignia and uniform of the German Kaiserreich.

"Verily!" Körner said with just the hint of a smile. He was part of the army corps the German General Staff had sent to Romania in order to chase out the Russians. Körner wore a black dolman with ribbon lacings and silver death's heads at the collar, the insignia of the Death's Heads Hussars. "We both seem to have been sent by our respective HQs to find quarters here," he continued. "Isn't that ironic, to say the least?"

"Indeed it is," Carl said. "How to solve this, then? Both staffs can hardly dwell here together."

"No, that would be a remarkable sight. However, as true gentlemen we'll have to solve it somehow. But for now let's eat, drink and be merry."

Soon a splendid dinner was served of grilled wild boar with sauce aux champignons and a good, red Burgundy wine in high goblets. Carl for his part eyed his peculiar host, the pale count. As intimated, he was chilled by his looks but Carl was also a gentleman.

"Excellent wine," he said, raising his glass to his host. "This is what you need after having been in the saddle all day."

The count thanked him and smiled his grinning, knowing smile. Carl thought that, well, maybe he wasn't so strange after all. We all have our quirks, looks and peculiarities. Meanwhile Madame Parysatis, for her part, was enjoying the meal. Having just devoured a well-boiled, wine-infused mushroom she turned to the count.

"Delighted! My compliments to the chef. Boar, is it?"

"Indeed," he replied, "hunted in these very grounds. Not by me personally, of course, as I have foresters in my service." Parysatis picked up on the hunting theme and asked Carl if he were a hunter.

"Actually, no. My brother back in Finland likes to hunt moose but I'm not into that at all."

"I see," the lady said. "But killing men is another matter?"

Carl smiled at her gentle challenge. "I defend the realm of the regime I serve. Of course I would prefer peace but if I'm ordered to fight the enemy, I fight. I'm no saint. I'm a man, no more and no less. And you, Madame…"

"Actually, it's Mrs."

"What is your husband's name, then, if I may enquire, so that I will know how to address you properly?"

"My husband's name is Morven."

At this, Körner, involuntarily drew in his breath. Körner served this Morven, who was a particularly sinister character of some importance to the unfolding situation. Körner of course knew Morven's wife, Parysatis, but he didn't want Carl to learn of this connection. Parysatis and the German had arrived separately at the castle but they were both there at Morven's instigation, Körner with orders to observe and report on the cosmic business there to take place and Parysatis to ensnare Carl with her charms. This strange meeting had come to pass because an angel, no less, had asked Count Alexandru to lend his castle for it, even encouraging the presence of Körner and Parysatis. As for Carl, he was to be the focal point of the coming showdown yet for now he knew nothing of such cosmic events. Just in order to be polite, Carl asked Parysatis who this Morven was.

"Oh, he's one of many talents, as am I," she replied casually. "We've been around for rather a long time, seeing generations and empires come and go. We've seen the struggle between the Light and the Dark. Personally, I can sometimes feel a bit fed up of the whole thing, this endless bickering between good and bad. Not my husband, though. He's a, shall we say, enthusiastic operator in the battles of the centuries."

At this she stopped, sensing that she had said too much. In a lighter vein, she added, "But don't call me 'Mrs Morven', although we are still married. Do call me Parysatis, please – only that – this is the name I usually go by."

Carl nodded, silently puzzled by the perspectives she hinted at, of 'having been around for a long time' and all that. But being a gentleman he didn't enquire further. "You are a very mysterious woman," was all he said.

"This I am," Parysatis remarked, knowing that Carl would be very surprised if he knew all about her. However, in due time he would get to know her true nature, and she would help him to see his own true nature too. Parysatis changed the subject and asked Körner what he felt about the sport of hunting. He said that he knew something of it but that he had no interest in it.

"Hunting is a sport, a game and a play," the German said, "and I don't have time for fun and games. Not that it's 'all work and no play' for me, no, for I have passion in everything that I do." Of course, Parysatis and Körner already knew one another and the woman well knew what the man would say, but she attempted to keep the conversation going.

"What's your passion, then?"

"To wage war, to fight and to kill," the German retorted. "That's what any true soldier likes and anyone denying it is a hypocrite."

"Is that true, Captain?" Parysatis turned to Carl. "Do soldiers love to fight and to kill?"

"In a way," Carl said thoughtfully. "You have to have some kind of inspiration in what you do. I know that to find pleasure in your work as a soldier might sound odd, but that's how it is. It's not a perfect world. There's war and strife. At the same time, we still want something better, right?"

"How do you mean?" Parysatis asked. "You're not a saint, you're a man as you just said."

Hearing this, Count Alexandru decided it was time to interpose. "But there is a need to strive for something better, as the captain admitted! As for myself, well I've been, how can I say, pretty much a 'grey area figure'. But now I try to improve upon my reputation, acting as a sort of esoteric ambassador and trying to brush up the façade, to start a new life. I try to be an ambassador with a view to mediate between good and evil. And for those interests I have another guest coming later this evening... um, an angel of sorts."

"An angel?" Körner almost exploded, looking angry. Morven had indeed told him that important events would take place at the castle, but of angels he had said nothing. Parysatis also reacted, her warm, bronze-red features paling a little. Even Carl started at the news, thinking that he, Carl, for instance liked reading about angels in the Bible – but was he ready to meet one in real life…?

"Indeed," the count said coolly. "I'm your host and I've been asked to lend my castle for a meeting of cosmic significance. If you don't like it, then leave."

Körner merely nodded at this. He wouldn't leave. And neither would Parysatis. Both of them served Morven who had told them to come here and play their parts in various ways.

"But more of this angelic affair later," their host continued. "Now let's finish our meal."

Carl and Körner bickered in a gentlemanly way over who would win the Romanian war, the Germans or the Russians, finally agreeing to disagree, both being practical military types not overly politically interested. At length, Carl laid down his silver cutlery, caught the last of the delicate sauce with a piece of bread, swallowed it and leaned back in his chair with its intricate woodwork. Putting his hands on his stomach, he praised the meal and his host, who in turn acknowledged him gracefully.

"Fine, thank you. And soon our fourth guest will arrive…"

"Aah, this angel fellow," Körner said, remembering his own secret task of observing and reporting on what would come to pass.

"Indeed," the count said. "I've invited another guest, a divine guest, in order for me to get some better karma and help me move a little more from the Dark towards the Light. Ending that grey area life and becoming a real individual, you know."

As if on cue, at this very moment the room was lit by a mild, golden-white light. Soon there emanated in the light a figure, a creature, a *gestalt* of supernatural splendour and charm. He had an ambiguous countenance, a silvery-grey lustre, a happy-yet-sad aura. In short, this was a melancholy angel. The figure's entrance was accompanied by music that sounded like a placid flute melody; however, it didn't come from any earthly instruments. The angel was clad in a blue-green gown with a golden belt and on his head he wore a frontlet with a silver medallion.

The people in the room reacted differently to this entrance. The count watched with mild interest, whilst Parysatis seemed a bit wary and Körner looked on in distinct dismay. Carl, for his part, being well versed in the Bible, was filled by a remarkable feeling, wondering if this really were an angel. Clues to this were the strange music and the soft light filling the room. Carl thought to himself, 'Well then, an angel it must be and I'm all for that, as the esoteric soldier I am'.

"Honoured angel," he said, "I'm at your service." He felt an irresistible urge to rise from the table and approach the angel, falling to his knees before it. The creature touched Carl's head and asked him to stand. "You are Carl Griffensteen," he said in a clear yet distant voice. "And I am Pelagion, a divine messenger and what is called a neutral angel. You did right in coming forth, since I have a message for you. I greet you and all the others gathered here tonight. I also thank Count Alexandru for inviting me."

The count, still seated as if frozen at the table like Körner and Parysatis, nodded at this. Then a silence ensued and Carl, standing next to the angel, took the opportunity to ask him what it meant to be a neutral angel. The being explained that when a certain upstart angel called Yaldabaoth had carried out a rebellion in Heaven, he had taken one third of the angel host with him. Another third remained loyal to God while the final third became neutral. Among these was Pelagion. Hearing this, Carl said that he understood. Indeed, he realised it all in a flash as the intuitive man he was. Being an esotericist also helped when meeting angels.

"We neutrals," the angel continued, "are used to mediate between good and bad, the Light and the Dark. And talking to humans is one of our tasks, to enter into a dialogue. Heaven's angels for their part don't converse, they only preach, being as they are on a higher plane, a higher and heavenly density sometimes called the fifth density. You are living on the third density. The dream world, or astral world, is the fourth. So I was sent to speak to you in order not to disturb you too much. I mean, you are pious and you have a creed, but I wouldn't think you're ready to meet the dwellers of the more sublime worlds yet."

The angel spoke with a mild, vaguely singing voice. It was indeed angelic but not distant and preaching, in other words a neutral voice. The other people in the room, the count, Parysatis and Körner, whether well-disposed or not, still merely looked on and let the show play out. Inevitably, Carl asked him why he had been sought out by the angel.

"You are going on a mission," Pelagion answered simply.

"I am?" Carl asked, taken aback. It would be his second mission within a few hours. "That sounds rather like an order to come from a neutral angel. Weren't you a creature of the discursive kind, one to enter into a dialogue?"

"True. You have free will, as do I, as do all beings everywhere. So then, what say you? Will you serve Heaven in a cosmically decisive quest?"

Carl, having set his mind long ago upon doing the Lord's bidding, was inwardly calm despite the enormity of the words. Yes, he was one who liked an adventure, especially if it could have some meaning to it: a fairy-tale adventure, a real adventure like the ones he had read about in his youth.

"I may well be ready to serve," he replied guardedly. "But first, tell me about the mission."

And so now the deva told him about finding The Rose That Never Fades. In order to find it, Carl would be translocated to another world, the astral world, the fourth density also known as The Land. It was all the same, the world of dreams and stories, of myths and legends. Pelagion said that this domain was very peculiar, being the expression of one's inner mind, of one's feelings and thoughts. To some extent the everyday world had the same quality, although not as directly as had this dream world. Among other things this meant that one didn't need any map in The Land, one only had to follow one's intuition and will. Still, if you got lost in spite of this, you could always ask your way from the beings you met. Venturing through The Land was about systematically relying on inner knowing, on the guidance of a higher lantern.

Carl fully understood this, and said as much to the angel. As for intuition, he had been guided by it often before; for example, when planning his army career he hadn't based it on any formal plans and considerations but on what he felt like doing. But now, as for this rather more profound mission, he needed to hear more. Pelagion complied.

"So then, if you would perform this task and you indeed find the Rose, after that you would go to the Flowery Meadow where I would tell you more. Clearly, it's a mission of gravity and great things are at stake – the world, the future of mankind, of freedom, of everything. It's about the victory of the Light. And first, it's about finding the Rose. This will serve, among other things, as a test for the rest of the undertaking. But I have to tell you that the aforementioned angel, the rebellious Yaldabaoth, is part of the equation too. To redeem him will be necessary. But to see if you're the right man for it all, first you have to find the Rose."

A dreamy Land, a Flowery Meadow, Heaven and Yaldabaoth. Carl thought that this sounded like a mission to his taste. And the other two dinner guests, Körner and Parysatis, were now listening very attentively. Körner, for his part, mused over the significance of the information, thinking that Morven wouldn't be at all pleased to hear this. Great things were indeed in the offing, no doubt about that, and cosmic events far bigger than the world war that was raging. But Parysatis was in two minds about it all, this mission presented to Carl and the moral dimension of it. Although somewhat estranged from Morven lately, she still loved her husband and remembered the task he had given her, that of ensnaring Carl. She would try to do that later, yet then on her own and not Morven's terms. Meanwhile, Carl liked the gist of the mission the angel had sketched but it still seemed rather vague to his practical mind.

"The Land, this is about going to The Land, you say. So how will I get there?"

"I will tell you soon," Pelagion said. "But first I have to ask whether you are ready? Will you accept the mission?"

Carl was in two minds. He was a Russian army captain out to recce cantonments for the staff. Then this heavenly proposal arrived. He wasn't happy about neglecting his army mission by accepting the quest for this Rose. However, in the face of an angel and his story, he just had to let it be. He made up his mind.

"Yes, I will. I shall do everything in my ability to solve the task. I want to assist Heaven in this work, first by finding the Rose and then meeting you at the Flowery Meadow to hear the rest of the mission."

"Fine," the angel said, nodding to him. "Here's your coat, cap and arms." A servant had already brought these items, as if the answer had been anticipated, and now handed them to Carl who put them on. "Now, go out to the yard," Pelagion continued. "There you will find your and Ivan's horses, dressed and watered and with full saddle bags. Now listen: ride towards the light. By this you will reach The Land I've spoken of. Ride for the sake of all that is good!"

With these words, the light in the room increased brilliantly and then slowly died out, as did the music. The neutral angel

Pelagion was gone. There only remained the now very pale host, his two other guests and Carl himself. Carl returned to his place at the table, somewhat agitated. Having calmed down he said to the Count, "So you really knew an angel was coming?"

"Yes," Alexandru said.

"And are you really a servant of Heaven?"

"Not really and I've never said that. I'm a middle man, enabling a cosmic event."

Carl nodded, remembering what the count had said about his condition. Still inquisitive Carl asked, "So then, the angel said that I should just go out to the yard and ride towards the light."

"Yes," the count agreed. "That sounds feasible. This is a special place, a nexus of realities. You'll see. So, you're off then? You are indeed going to The Land, doing the angel's bidding just like that?"

"Yes," Carl said. "This feels right."

"Well then, you're a bit like me," the count said, "just doing it, just going on your way with no broodings, no calculations. You just go and see what happens."

"Something like that," Carl mused. He couldn't help himself adding a Napoleon quotation, *On s'engage et puis on verra.*"

"First you engage," Körner observed, finally having something to relate to after all this divine spectacle, "then you have a look around. A fine operational motto."

Carl nodded and rose to leave. Parysatis also rose and approached him, remembering her task to ensnare the man.

"Indeed, you're off to The Land. I wish you well, in a way. Now remember, in fact I have a castle in The Land, Hortalion by name, a charming estate with walls of bronze, resplendent golden halls and a lovely garden. Stop by there, if you wish, and we can have a good time…"

Carl nodded, for the moment amorous play being far from his mind. Still, she was a beauty. "Thank you, my lady. You never know, we may meet again in this world or another."

"No meeting is the first and no farewell is the last."

The count wished him luck while Körner just nodded at him. Strange, Carl wondered, does he have some ulterior motive behind his stern military face? Or is it just the political enmity of German versus Russian? Körner, for his part, decided to keep silent about his next move, to go and seek out Morven and report on the cosmic meeting having just taken place.

CHAPTER THREE

THE LAND

A servant led Carl out into the courtyard, lit only by a full moon. There Ivan met up with his master, telling him about having had a fine meal and then suddenly receiving orders to pack and meet him here.

"Fine, Sergeant," Carl said. "We're going on another mission now, a mission beyond the beyond. Are you in? I wouldn't blame you if you're not. This is truly a gamble. But it is, I promise you, a mission from God – to find something called The Rose That Never Fades. Then we'll go on to redeem some wayward angel, as I understand it."

Ivan looked at him with a serious, completely bemused expression.

"A mission from God… finding a rose… redeeming a devil…?" he responded finally. But then it only took a moment for him to decide. "Well, bless me, I'm all for that! I will serve with you, Captain. The army service aside, I'm also a Christian soldier willing to do His bidding. This is my statement before Heaven and Earth. I will come along."

This settled, they mounted their horses. Slowly crossing the yard, a light suddenly appeared, a portal of shimmering golden light. It was the light that the angel had spoken of, the light they had to ride into. This they did, calmly but with dedicated spirits. And suddenly they were through and enveloped by a complete change of scenery: the moment before they had been in a Transylvanian courtyard in an autumn night, now they were out in a summery glade with the sun beating down and birds singing.

"What the…?" exclaimed Ivan. "A moment ago it was night, now it's broad daylight."

"Indeed," Carl said, attempting to explain the nature of The Land, the astral realm they were in, a psychological landscape adapting to their inner minds.

"A dream world, eh?" Ivan said. "A fairy land, sort of? Then we're the knight and his groom! How fitting."

"Yes," Carl said, "though a knight in a grey uniform with a sabre and a Nagant revolver."

"Ladies and gentlemen, I give you – the Grey Knight," Ivan said, half in jest.

"The Grey Knight," Carl repeated. "Now doesn't that sound sweet and yet sober, a fitting title for me on this quest. A soldier of the twentieth century going off in an imaginary world to seek a Rose, then on to redeem the world. It's kind of crazy, kind of impossible. But long live the impossible freedom!"

Shouting this old mercenary motto, Carl rode away from the clearing, followed by his groom and ADC. Following his intuition, he just rode on, the landscape of The Land adapting to his mind. It was an expression of the mind, so that you never needed maps, you just let your inner light guide you. It was, Carl reasoned, a question of, 'Si tuum psyche requiris, circumspice': if you want to see your inner mind, look around.

They rode through a hardwood forest, the ground covered by white flowers. Ivan looked around himself in amazement.

"So where are we – and when do we eat?" He was always hungry.

Carl again explained the metaphysics of The Land, it being a realisation of their inner thoughts and visions. The Land lay apparently tangible before their eyes, with trees and grass and sky and all, and personally they still had their human needs of food and drink. But now the latter were mostly figments of the mind, hunger and thirst not essentially part of this immaterial but spiritual domain. However, it was only the fourth density, not the fifth, so thoughts of hunger and thirst still existed here. Indeed, thirst existed here now, as they approached a brook lined by birches.

They let their horses enter the shallow stream, the riders dismounting and filling their water bottles. Ivan for his part took his aluminium bottle, removing the protective grey cloth and submerging the bottle in the stream, filling it and raising it to his lips to drink. He sat on a stone by the stream as if sunbathing.

"So we're out to find this rose, some eternal rose. Where to, then?"

"I'll think of something," Carl said, reminding himself that he could always ask the way if he didn't know where to go. As if to himself, he repeated the ontology of this place. "We'll have to realise the Rose within, somehow. Then we'll find it. Or not!"

To be sure, Ivan didn't get the meaning of this. He had a simple nature, content with having an adventure to experience, a good horse to carry him and a knight to serve. And these he had.

Just then an enigmatic being passed over them in the sky, a long, green creature with lazily flapping, bat-like wings and the unmistakable look of a dragon. Carl watched it pass dreamily. He even thought that he could see a rider on its back and was enchanted by the vision of a dragon ride for a dream traveller, gliding over The Land like an uncrowned king of the skies. He wondered why it made him feel uneasy, but let the thought go. Ivan also cast a glance at the pair but he wasn't so carried away.

"Some kind of lizard, eh?"

Having crossed the brook they continued along the road ahead, enjoying the weather and the birds singing. Before long they met a farmer, a bearded yeoman of the astral world, and Carl took the opportunity to ask him where The Rose That Never Fades could be sought; he told them to go to a town called Gremoburg.

"Gremoburg? Indeed?" Carl repeated.

"You can at least try there," the farmer said. "I don't exactly know how you'll find what you're asking for, I only recall that there's some connection to the Rose in that town." Pressed for more information, the farmer said that Gremoburg was a mountain town. And how to find it? By intuition, this Carl knew by now. He thanked the man and the pair then rode on to Gremoburg.

Following winding paths and turning when it seemed right, they slowly rode towards their goal through a landscape of meadows and pastures, of groves and flowers basking in the sun. Canola seemed to be a common crop, a golden yellow rapeseed from which one presses oil. It grew both in the fields and wildly sown in the road ditches.

Thus, while everything seemed to be going well for the two brave adventurers, the dragon, the one they had just seen, did indeed have a rider on its back and he was none other than Maximilian Körner, the German officer met at Count Alexandru's castle. And having followed them into the light and searched the skies of The Land, he had spotted the pair on their astral quest.

Körner, the German vanguard commander who happened to end up in the same castle as the Finlander during that Romanian campaign, was now bent on stopping him. It was Morven who had ordered Körner to be there. The very first meeting between Körner and Morven had taken place before the war, one spring day in 1913, when the German had unexpectedly been visited by a bald man in a grey cassock, a quirky monk-type with a sturdy build and fine manners. What had struck Körner most was the man's constant grimace, a pained expression resulting in the constant exposure of his teeth. He called himself Morven.

Having been invited into Körner's apartment in Friedrichsfelde, in East Berlin, Morven accepted a glass of Weissbier. This bright beer was perhaps an odd choice for an adept with dark leanings. The Erik Karlfeldt line *'sub luna bibo, dark is my brew'*, springs to mind as more fitting for this twilight figure. Morven had an offer for the cavalryman and soon came straight to the point.

"Come into the service of me and my Lord, that is, Prince Yaldabaoth, known as Lucifer."

"And why should I do this?" the German had asked, reasonably.

"Because if you do, you would get command of large units, you would experience victory and carnage on a cosmic scale and you would see battle like never before. You'll see triumph and tragedy, change and adventure. You'll have it all and then some, more than anything you could have in this world. Are you in?"

After only a little hesitation, realising that he would continue to serve in the German army while also serving Morven, Körner agreed to the offer. What dark-minded soldier would not want to become a true warlord, a lord of devastated worlds, of this world and the next? Körner thus entered Morven's service, swearing obedience to him.

Not long after this, he was led through a dimensional portal to The Land and to Morven's Wooden Castle. Once there, Körner was initiated into another secret, namely that he, Körner, had been a soldier in several previous lives, in life after life. He had settled on the samsara journey of the archetypal Dark Knight, having in fact been in the service of Morven throughout history, serving this curious master as executioner, robber baron and warrior. And he had loved it. The visit to his Berlin apartment in this current life was just to remind him of what had always been, a reminder of his true self.

After a sojourn in The Land on various missions, Körner had returned to the pre-war world of 1913, no time having elapsed during his travels away. He had resumed his Rittmeister life, doing his duty as an officer, and after about a year he got the war that he had always secretly longed for, the Great War. In the Imperial German Army he fought by the Masurian Lakes and in Silesia and rose through the ranks to lieutenant colonel. Finally he commanded the advance guard battalion of the army corps that Mackensen led into Romania. And thus, at Morven's instigation, he came to visit Alexandru's castle apparently to recce cantonments, just as Griffensteen did for his unit.

What Körner had witnessed there, with Pelagion and all that supposedly divine apparition and music, still rankled in his mind. Personally, Körner had disliked Pelagion's performance. Nor did the gist of the angel's sermon inspire or please Körner, as the Dark Knight he was. And true to his promise to Morven, he would have to tell him everything about this, tell his master that the Light was on the march. Of course, he couldn't just write a letter for Morven lived in the strange dimensions of The Land and its parallel world. But he had instructed Körner what to do in order to make contact, by pronouncing a certain spell.

At Castle Munte, Körner had watched Carl leave. The German for his part remained in the dining hall to finish his food and wine, then excused himself to Parysatis and the count saying that he had 'business' to attend to.

Only Alexandru and Parysatis remained. The count knew Parysatis like she knew Körner, superficially, having met perhaps once or twice in the mysterious confluences of parallel worlds. Now, sitting in the very material dining hall where servants were cleaning the table, Alexandru pondered the recent events.

"Both the Russian and the German came here to organise cantonments," he observed, "but nobody seems to have bothered to fix that."

Parysatis drank her wine and nodded.

"There were obviously more important things to do," she replied, and Alexandru smiled.

"Maybe so. It seems as though forces are gathering for a dance, a demonic dance in the far dimensions, a Shiva dance in the omniverse of samsara. Perhaps my guests are both key players in this... and maybe even you and I?"

"You never know," said Parysatis. "I mentioned earlier that I myself have a castle in The Land that Pelagion talked about. You might know it?"

"Yes," said Alexandru, "The Land, I know a little of it, having been there a few times. What was your place called again?"

"Hortalion, the Bronze Castle. Stop by if you're in the neighbourhood." The count bowed in thanks to the lady for this invitation while Parysatis went on, "Griffensteen has a mission in The Land. So I guess Körner is going there too."

"How do you know that?" her host asked, still unaware of the events he had unwittingly set in motion. "I mean, true, Griffensteen did receive a mission there, this we heard – but Körner?"

"I can feel it," Parysatis said. "The Land is a dimension of crossroads, being bordered by other countries of both time and space, an intermediate zone between all other worlds. And, well, I know this and that. And I've come across Körner before because he serves my husband, Morven. Körner is an experienced man in the ins and outs of The Land."

"The Land," said the count dreamily as he drank his wine. "Who can tell what is now taking place in that magical place? I myself have flown there as a night swallow on occasion, taking shortcuts across its nightly climes." He was trying to flirt with his dinner companion. "So maybe I would indeed fly to your castle sometime..."

Parysatis looked mischievously at him with narrowed eyes over her glass. "As I said, you're most welcome, my dear Count."

Her answer was merely due to the demands of courtesy for she was more interested in Captain Griffensteen, at Morven's demand but even more so now that she had met him: the noble warrior, the Grey Knight with eyes of steel and heroic countenance, a gust of wind from the Hyperborean north.

Morven was indeed a cunning operator and he had his ways of obtaining information. In his crystal he had seen that Carl Griffensteen would be heading for Castle Munte, and other sources had suggested that there were plans to give the man an astral assignment, a quest for the Light. This could only affect Morven adversely. Thus he used his influence to have his trusted lieutenant Körner, already taking part in the Romanian campaign, present at the castle; Morven also sent his wife there to do what came naturally to her.

As Parysatis finished her glass her thoughts turned to the near future. As soon as she came back to The Land she must entice Griffensteen to her in some way, lure him to her castle. Perhaps the pleasure of her company would lead him to destruction, turning him to the darkness and to serve more sinister fellows. Yet in her heart she didn't actually feel this, she was tired of all this darkness and despair. Maybe instead she could lead him on to clarity. And beyond that, maybe even love him on his own terms?

She sighed to herself and told her host that she would withdraw for the night. The gentleman that he was, the count didn't try to dissuade her. As part of his reconciliation with better powers, his old philandering days were over.

Körner had excused himself from the castle hall, gone to his room and girded himself with a sword, then put on the fur coat and hat with the skull emblem of the Death's Head Hussars he belonged to. Next he went down to the stables, mounted his red roan and rode away into the night. Having gone some way out of sight of Castle Munte he reined in the horse, cleared his throat and began to sing an incantation that Morven had taught him. He sang in a loud, clear voice in the moonlight, and in a moment the nearby rocks themselves opened, a portal lined with sparks opening out of nowhere. Körner urged on his steed and rode into the crack, this portal to the other world, The Land. More great sparks flew up as the gate closed again with a bang, leaving no trace.

Maximilian Körner rode between the worlds, travelling between dimensions. He rode, as it were, through a strange, spacious, luminous cave that eventually led him out onto a twilight plain that soon evolved into a forest, a dark and dripping forest with gnarled roots, scurrying vermin and laughing trolls. Dark ponds mirrored the blackness of the skies, deepening it. The forest was called Nicky Woods.

Going ever deeper through the forest, Körner suddenly heard the murmur of a brook and followed it until he saw his goal, a castle of wood in the middle of the forest. It was a stately, barbaric structure of tarred timbers and lacquered planks, a veritable tower with recesses and protrusions all adorned with carvings of plant and animal ornamentation. It had red shutters and windows of bottle glass, soldered with lead. Körner crossed the creek on a wooden bridge, reined in the horse and dismounted, letting the horse go to drink at the stream while he himself went up the steps to the castle entrance and hammered on the solid doors with the iron knocker. He was eventually let inside by a servant, a tall figure with a long, aquiline nose, a striped, pointed cap on his head and clothes of red and green. This was Ringo Badger, Morven's butler and handyman.

"Aah, Lieutenant Colonel Körner," said the man. "Such an honour."

"Thank you, Badger," replied Körner and gave the servant his busby and fur-lined jacket. "So is all well with our lord?"

"As good as it gets," Badger said casually.

"How so?"

"He always seems so, well, pained."

"You mean, like, tormented?" Körner asked. "Passionate, I would probably call it."

The man with the pointed cap shrugged. Then he led the guest into a vestibule; there was a bearskin on the floor and hunting weapons on the walls. "But can he laugh?" Badger mused. "Man is the *animal risible*, 'the animal who laughs', but does our venerable lord know what laughter is?"

"A fine observation," Körner agreed. "One must be able to laugh. If one is human, that is. Morven is perhaps human but he's more than that."

They passed through the castle's chambers, along its aisles and corridors and up its staircases. Somewhat later Körner stood in a wood-panelled salon with a silk rug and on one wall a large oil painting depicting two moose in a pine forest, all lit by candles in cast iron brackets. Opposite him sat Morven in an embroidered kaftan, smiling that constant, ambiguous smile.

"So what news?" Morven said, his old master of the dark side. "Why are you here?" He waved an arm to indicate a chair for his visitor.

"Something alarming has happened," Körner said as he settled. "The forces of the Light have acquired a new champion."

Morven raised an eyebrow. He wasn't completely surprised by this, having observed events unfolding earlier as the Russian army captain made his way to Castle Munte. "So this neophyte of theirs is Carl Griffensteen?"

"Yes, and he's in the service of Heaven now, on a quest to redeem Lucifer himself!"

"Indeed? But how will he do that?"

Körner told his master what he had witnessed in Alexandru's dining hall, about Pelagion's unexpected appearance and what the angel had said to Griffensteen.

"Dire tidings," Morven muttered, deliberating on this new offensive, this spiritual onslaught aimed at redeeming Yaldabaoth, his own master in turn. "This is what I've always been afraid of, that Heaven would employ such a man in this position, allowing his free will to work in cosmic favour. I sense bad things, a crucial setback for our forces. This must be stopped. Carl Griffensteen must be intercepted, yes, in fact killed. Free will is the worst thing there is, that someone could spontaneously choose the Light. It's the worst of all threats to our camp." He paused, grimacing, teeth bared. "You have to stop him, Max. Well, do you have any ideas?"

"Indeed I do," Körner said without hesitation, having thought of little else on his journey here.

"Good. So what's the plan?"

"Well," said Körner, "for one thing, I know a certain mechanic who fabricates birds -"

"Eh? Birds?"

"Yes, metal birds, creatures with a great wingspan and long, sharp claws. They can be trained to dive in attack. I can go and organise this if only I may borrow some transport?"

"Of course, you may borrow my wyvern."

Körner knew of these creatures, huge bipedal flying lizards, having flown them before in The Land. Morven then also gave the German a pocket crystal that could be used to locate Carl's whereabouts.

After some refreshments they went out together to a clearing in the forest where the extraordinary lizard dwelled; it was already furnished with saddle and harness. The scales of the creature shimmered in emerald green and blue, its open beak bared sharp teeth and the black ellipsoidal pupils of its snake-like eyes looked inscrutably at its prospective rider. Körner walked up to the animal, patted it and talked kindly to it, as kindly as he was capable. As soon as he had been accepted, he mounted the beast, said goodbye to the adept and took to the skies with leathery wings.

CHAPTER FOUR
AERIAL ATTACK

Körner mounted the lizard and flew away over the green expanses of Nicky Woods. It was truly a sight for the gods: a German officer in black uniform with skull-embossed fur hat, a man riding a fabulous, mythological winged beast.

Once airborne, Körner took out the crystal and gazed into it, concentrating mentally on the figure of Carl. He saw moving images beginning to appear in the misty depths of the object, finally giving him a glimpse of his adversary and his whereabouts. Steering his powerful mount in the estimated direction, Körner flew across endless expanses of verdant moorland and lush woodland under the midday sun, though to his eyes the landscape appeared grey and uninteresting. Then searching the ground he soon saw two riders, one on a brown horse and the other on a black one. From a case Körner wore over the shoulder he produced a pair of Zeiss binoculars, standard German army issue in 1917. Only a quick look was required to affirm that it was Carl with a companion.

"Excellent!" Körner said under his breath, pleased with himself to have it confirmed that his adversary was indeed in The Land. Now the German veered away through the sky to another neighbourhood, a forest where lived the mechanic who would arrange the deadly metal birds. This man was named Bestos Fokalion. Over The Land, over forests and lakes, mountains and heaths he rode until at length he reached his goal in a particular coniferous forest set on a flat land with great expanses of pine trees. Soon he saw an impressive complex among the trees, a gathering of buildings with slate roofs and wooden outbuildings, his target. Hovering over a large clearing he ordered the lizard to land. Once on the ground Körner set out across a dull, worn grassy field, soon spotting the mechanic's house and walking towards it.

The impressive main building was of green marble, though having a rather sombre look to it with its barred windows. Without further ado Körner approached the porch stairs, ascended, knocked on the door and went inside even though no-one came to open. There were no servants here, Fokalion being a secretive chap. Eventually he found himself standing in a room full of contraptions and gadgets, the walls lined with bizarre machines and sinister automata, adorned with silver and platinum and precious stones such as agate and jasper. In addition to this there were three parallel workbenches in the middle of the room, cluttered with lesser objects: gears, nuts, washers, rods, bolts, clockworks, switchgear, hoses, pipes, pumps, flywheels and drive belts. The surfaces glistened with brass, steel and bronze, and smelled of oil, fuels and turpentine. Ameliorating the somewhat titanic nature of the place, surprisingly, was soft music coming from the far end of the room where a man was standing bent over some work.

Körner cleared his throat and approached. The figure at the workbench raised his head and glanced at the newcomer from beneath overgrown eyebrows.

"Bestos Fokalion, maker of strange thingamajigs, how are you?"

"Oh, it's you, my friend," the man said absentmindedly, returning to his work. He was dressed in a well-worn, oil-stained leather apron and a leather hood, his face a pattern of grime-engrained wrinkles. The music came from a self-playing barrel organ on the bench, a neat machine in green and red with a loudspeaker decorated with gothic tracery. When Körner came up to stand beside Bestos he saw that he was working on a doll, a one metre long mannequin with a genuine human look to it; its face was carved of wood yet the eyes moved naturally, now meeting Körner's gaze. The German fixedly looked back at the doll, seeing the glint in the artificial eyes. They stared at each other for a few seconds, then the doll lowered its eyes. Having won this battle of wills, the German relaxed.

"Some fascinating workshop you have here, Bestos."

"Mmm," muttered the other, closing a gap on the dummy's stomach and securing it with a latch before putting down his screwdriver and glancing at his visitor. "So then, Mr Max, why are you here?"

"I'm here to admire your work," Körner said, "especially the birds."

"Which birds are they?"

"The, hmm, special metal birds."

At this the mechanic smiled and said, "Aah, *those* metal birds. You ordered them quite a long time ago but never turned up."

"True," agreed Körner. He had once asked Bestos to invent and produce some mechanical fighting birds that he would need for a particular purpose during a previous stay in The Land, to be used in an earlier dispute. However, that argument had unfortunately been resolved in a peaceful way.[1]

Bestos waved to Körner to follow him. They left the workshop, came out into a courtyard lined with houses built of slag brick, arrived at a vault, went through a green door and came to a lofty barn where they stopped. There, on a floor of wooden planks, stood eight metal birds, each one more than a metre tall and with folded wings. They had bodies of plated silver, huge steel claws

---

[1]   It was the affair of the Grapasias' Mysterious Fountains, which might be worth telling another time.

and wings of bronze tipped with platinum. The eyes were of ruby, glowing with artificial life. Körner approached the creatures with some devotion.

"Sweet! Soon they'll all follow my commands!"

"Indeed," said Bestos, "with a special flute that I'll show you."

"Aha. So I have to be with them myself?"

"Oh yes, you must. You'll have to fly on an eagle, or whatever."

"That'll be alright. I have that covered," said Körner, telling the man about the wyvern. "Right now I have an urgent job for these beauties."

Bestos nodded and said, "We'd better get started, then."

He snapped his fingers and suddenly a gap opened up in the roof of the barn, with large sheets of steel slipping away on well-oiled rails. Then the mechanic took from a locked cabinet to one side a small flute that he blew, a clear tone in D major. Immediately the birds started to move, spreading their wings and rising one by one, circling inside the spacious barn so that Körner had to duck his head. Eventually the creatures flew out through the hole in the roof.

Bestos hurried out of the barn, heading for a certain meadow where he continued to blow different tunes with the flute. The birds seemed to move as one according to the sounds. Körner at last caught up with Bestos and was taught the flute's melodies. It wasn't long before he was able to direct the birds himself so he made them land, reaching out his hand to say thanks to Bestos. The mechanic took it and shrugged humbly, playing down his role, but Körner would have none of it.

"No, this is important! You have done a great job. With these birds I'm going to stop a very dangerous fellow, an enemy who works against me, no, against all of us pledged to the Dark."

"Oh, indeed? Then it really is important. Who's this enemy?"

"A man who rides for the Light, a Russian knight of sorts, looking for a special rose."

"A knight? In service of the Light, you say? This sounds awful. I mean, obscurity is our way, twilight and shadow are the thing. There can be nothing better than to sit at dusk with a keg of wine and watch countries burning in the last rays of the sun."

"True," said Körner, "and the delight of devilry in the stillness of the night, howling beneath the moon on a mission to shed blood."

"We seem to be of the same spirit," said Bestos. "For me, life's great pleasure is to stand forging in the night hours and watch the sparks fly, to build monstrous machines of enslavement, to have the smell of explosives in the nostrils and see my fingers glow with sheer creativity. Such joy!"

He wished his customer and comrade good luck. Körner again thanked the man, excused himself and retraced his steps back to the clearing where the wyvern waited faithfully with raised head. Körner for his part approached carefully – one must always be circumspect with such wild creatures – and greeted the beast, got into the saddle without ceremony and flew back to the meadow where the metal flock waited. They circled over it for a while and then he blew a specific sequence on the flute. Immediately the birds started to move with gentle rattling and creaking sounds, rising into the sky as one. Gaining altitude, they formed themselves into a veritable squadron, a plough formation in the wake of Körner on his wyvern. With each bird having a wingspan of three metres it was an impressive and terrible sight.

From his inside pocket Körner again produced the crystal, concentrated on Carl and soon saw his misty image take form within. The German intuitively estimated the direction to take and steered his aerial company there for a deadly rendezvous.

By this time Carl and Ivan were riding through a bright landscape scattered with groves of aspen and maple, gleaming emerald green under the sun. Small fluffy clouds drifted across the sky. Their goal was Gremoburg, the place where the farmer had told them some information about the Rose was to be found. It had been a peaceful ride on a peaceful day, but this came to an abrupt end when Ivan cast a glance up into the skies, seeing Körner at the back of his lizard. He had spotted him before, the curious beast scouting its way high in the air perhaps with a lone rider on board. But now it was followed by eight giant metal birds, their wings glistening in the sun.

"What in Heaven's name is that?" Ivan said, pointing.

Carl looked up and paled; it was again the dragon he had seen when they first came to The Land, this time however with an entire flight formation, the huge animal with a black-uniformed rider and its entourage of ungodly mechanical things. Before he could say anything, Körner had blown his flute and part of the squadron came diving down towards them, four birds in a vanguard.

Instinctively, the officer that he was, Carl gathered himself quickly and ordered Ivan in his usual penetrating if a little hoarse voice, "Present arms!"

Ivan obeyed, pulling his Nagant from the holster on his belt. Carl drew his own gun and took aim.

"Shoot when they are less than fifty metres away, preferably closer!"

"When I see the whites of their eyes," Ivan said, confirming that he had understood, while wondering whether these things even had eyes. They sat still in the saddle and let the birds dive, carefully watching their golden, silvery and bronze splendour shine in the sun, simply allowing their arrow-shaped forms to rush forward and approach them at speed with swept-back wings. At the last moment, the birds spread their wings, thrusting forward their huge claws to attack the men.

Carl shot at the nearest bird. It was hit, yawed a bit, lost the glow in its ruby eyes and then flew on and plummeted into the ground some distance behind the black stallion. He cocked his gun and fired another shot which wounded a bird in the wing. Meanwhile Ivan had downed a bird too. The fourth flew back up to its peers, who circled in readiness. And soon the four who hadn't been tried in battle yet came in together for a joint attack.

Ivan and Carl prepared themselves for the worst, yet were still battle-eager and with weapons at the ready. In the ensuing fray, the captain's uniform was torn by a bird's claw and Ivan narrowly avoided having his head ripped open. Soon they were both shooting in partnership at their assailants, two shots for each bird. The birds were close and their bullets didn't miss, still it took some presence of mind for the men to shoot straight in this calamity.

When only two birds remained, they gave up their attempted attack and returned above to their master, giving the soldiers an opportunity to reload. Carl found that he had now run out of spare ammunition, his pockets empty.

"Do you have cartridges to lend me, striker?"

"Funnily enough, no!" Ivan replied.

It might be thought that this shouldn't have presented a problem, if The Land were a mental projection, a place where all was of the mind; surely Carl and Ivan could simply intend more ammunition by their will? The trouble was that, in the heat of battle with terrible creatures never before encountered, it never entered their minds to perform such a feat. They weren't that proficient in the ways of The Land. So now they had to rely on their sabres.

Hovering in the air above, Körner saw with some dismay his two birds return and rejoin the one who had got away in the first attack, now repairing itself. He now launched a final assault with the remaining birds, to be met by Ivan and Carl with drawn sabres. The blades flashed and thrust in skilled hands with a clash of steel against steel, resulting in two more birds brought down and only one making it back to his master. In disbelief, then Körner steered his lizard away from the scene, followed by his one remaining, badly damaged, creaking metal bird. Down on the ground, the exhausted soldiers watched the flight disappear away and over the horizon.

"There was a man on the back of the lizard-thing," panted Ivan.

"Indeed there was," Carl said. "And I'm sure he looked like Maximilian Körner."

"Who's that?"

Carl then told Ivan about the German he had dined with at Castle Munte. Ivan had eaten in the kitchen and so had been unaware of the hussar and, indeed, the other enigmatic guests. While they continued towards Gremoburg, Carl privately pondered over the meaning of this latest encounter, wondering what Körner's presence in The Land could mean.

CHAPTER FIVE

GREMOBURG

Körner had one more ace up his sleeve in trying to stop Carl and Ivan, one more way of attacking them directly though not in person, which he deemed risked suicide. He was brave but he wasn't foolish, which facing two armed combat veterans in a face-to-face scuffle would be. But he had the advantage of having been in The Land many times and had no less than a monster in his service – like attracts like, as it were – a certain four-armed beast living in a swamp. To get in touch with this he had to leave the wyvern on a nearby meadow, the two creatures being somewhat at odds. Two monsters in the same place isn't a winning combination. Besides it would be hard to land the lizard in the wet fenlands he was going to.

Having come to earth, Körner ventured over bogs and morasses and through deciduous forests and thickets, the sky grey and dull. Soon he came upon the monster's lair, a large hut, an impressive heap of intertwined logs and branches forming a small hill with the entrance like a virtual cave, the opening being several metres in diameter. Not daring at first to venture inside, Körner halted before the cave and spoke in the kindest, friendliest voice he could muster.

"Quriti, are you there? My giant friend, are you sleeping or awake? I have a proposal for you." From inside the hut a growl was heard.

"What's that?" came a strong, guttural voice in reply. "Someone speaks my name. Who is it?"

"It's me, Max Körner."

"Indeed? That seems like good tidings, if you have work for me."

From inside the structure a giant now emerged, a four and a half metres tall, hairy monster like a giant gorilla except for the four massive arms and bald head, the face dominated by a long nose and a wide mouth baring sharp fangs. The eyes were slanted and had a peculiar spark in them, somehow not altogether as evil as one might expect from such a threatening countenance. Körner involuntarily backed off before this appearance, this towering ogre.

"Max Körner! Yes, I remember you. You helped me once, pulling a thorn from my foot."

"Indeed I did," the German said. "And you promised me a favour in return. Now I'm here to redeem it."

He then described the mission he had in mind, for killing Carl Griffensteen. When the monster asked when and where this could be done, Körner again took out his crystal to locate Carl's whereabouts. The captain and his aide were now riding through a treeless area so Körner decided that the attack would have to wait for a moment when they rode through a forest or the like, where Quriti could ambush them more easily.

Specifically, the pair were riding across a certain open plateau bordered by colossal mountains. The weather was clear, thin clouds floated high above and in the distance the plain faded in a haze. Suddenly, scouting a little way ahead, Ivan caught sight of something and pointed to one of the mountains.

"Look there, a city!"

"Indeed," said Carl. "It must be Gremoburg."

It was a city atop a mountain, a city of red and ruddy brown houses, basking in the sun; in the centre could be seen a white keep and a donjon with a tower from which a banner flew. The mountainside glowed with greenish rocks. They rode on towards it, found a road that led up the mountainside and followed its meandering path. However, at closer range the green colour of the rocks faded, becoming a more common grey; here, the curves were steep, the path running on narrow shelves where high cliffs towered over the riders.

Outside the closed city gates, as if waiting for them, stood a man almost two metres tall and wearing a violet tunic, burgundy trousers and black boots and on his head a tricorne hat. He had a peculiar face, with protruding cheekbones and a pointed chin, yet he exuded understated strength and a quiet calm.

"Greetings! I'm Krygon, Custodian of Gremoburg, the ruler of this fair city. Who are you?"

"Pilgrims, sir," Carl answered.

"Pilgrims with swords?"

"We are spiritual soldiers," Carl continued, "in search of The Rose That Never Fades. We've heard that information about it might be found in your city."

Krygon thought about this for a moment, deciding to trust the visitors. "Ah, the Rose..." he then mused. "As I remember, there are some lines about it in the Book of the Worlds, a tome to be found in the castle library. You are welcome to go and search it. Just tell the castellan that I've given you my permission."

Krygon signalled for the gate to be opened and the two travellers thanked him profusely and rode into the city, along steep alleyways and up to a plaza. At the square they had a closer look at the castle, its white-plastered stone walls rising high and impregnable. Small window openings with round arches looked out onto the square.

"Here is our goal, then," Carl said. "The castle with its library."

Ivan was sent to buy some bread and apples and arrange for the horses to be watered and groomed in a stable, while his master sought an audience in the castle. With his honest, open countenance Carl convinced the palace guard officer that he was who he said he was, a man who wanted to search the library for some esoteric information. The castellan, a grave, black-clad fellow, came out to meet him and led him into the castle and up to the library, housed in a tower chamber with painted panels, arched windows and two upholstered chairs at a table. There were shelves along all four walls, covered with scrolls and bound volumes.

Before long, Ivan arrived too and sat himself in one of the chairs. "We're lucky this is a small library!" he observed. "Probably it won't take too long to go through it."

"Agreed," said Carl. "So let's get started right away!"

"Can't I eat an apple first, at least? It's been a long ride, not to mention the fight."

"Sure. Give me one too."

They took out their knives and peeled the apples that Ivan had bought, then got to grips with finding the Book of the Worlds, the tome that they hoped would contain some information about the Rose. After some time perusing the shelves, it was found, a thick volume with covers of silver plate. Having skimmed its pages for the word 'Rose', Carl finally gathered that a further clue to its whereabouts was to be found in something called the City of Gold. Ivan expressed surprise that this knowledge was found so easily in the very large book, and Carl took the opportunity to explain again about how one's mentality worked here: he was focused on the Rose, of a positive mind and he knew that his quest could be completed. The Land was a place of the mind, a mental projection, and the ease with which they progressed was an example of that.

It was decided not to waste any more time here but to ride on to the City of Gold. So they left the castle, went to the stables to fetch their horses and rode back to the gate. Outside it, Krygon was now sitting bareheaded on a stool, basking in the sun. When he saw the pair he put on his hat and gathered himself up.

"Ah, the armed pilgrims. Did you find what you were looking for?"

As an experienced military man, Carl believed in operational security, not giving out information to people who weren't involved in one's mission. Security had to be tight, in The Land no less than in the everyday world. However, his intuition told him that Krygon was a man of the right kind, a soulful man, a man of the Light.

"Indeed, I found what I was looking for," he agreed, "a clue to the whereabouts of The Rose That Never Fades." Krygon nodded and wished them luck with their quest, blessing them for the spiritual intentions that he perceived.

"Thank you," Carl said. "You're a man after my own heart, perhaps another knight of the Light?"

"Maybe I am," Krygon observed. "So if you need my help at some point, just come by here again."

"I'll keep that in mind," Carl said. "Until then, good fortune with your affairs, may the Light guide you and your people."

"We'll do that," smiled Krygon and resumed his sunbathing.

Thus they left Krygon, Carl sensing that indeed they would meet him again later. The pair rode away from Gremoburg, down the serpentine road and away across the plain where they eventually spent the night in the open.

After riding over barren heathland and desert climes, Ivan and Carl finally ventured into a lush oak forest. Within moments they were stopped in their tracks by Quriti, the giant, hairy ogre with four arms and a fearsome countenance that Körner had summoned to attack them. While remaining back at the monster's hut, Körner had followed the progress of the pair through his crystal, seeing at last that they had ridden into a forest suitable for the ambush. Thus, eventually, the creature could now emerge on the path in front of them, their escape blocked by the oaks. Carl found himself standing before a nightmare, but he quickly gathered himself.

"Who are you? Speak, in the name of God!" he ordered in a strong voice that betrayed no fear. When the beast heard that phrase 'in the name of God' it had, like all other beings of the omniverse, high and low, good and evil, to answer.

"I'm Quriti, a great monster sent to kill you."

"Well," said Carl, thinking fast, "go on, do it then."

"I will!" Quriti bellowed, raising his four arms as a dark glow appeared in his eyes.

Yet Carl remained perfectly calm, not letting his soul catch fire, not allowing any passion to flare up, so as to reach out with his mind and link with the monster's aura. This unexpected behaviour made the beast hesitate, so Carl seized the opportunity.

"My friend, don't you know that what you're doing is useless here? Come on now, calm down. It doesn't have to be like this. Try lifting your head up freely and breathing deeply."

To its own surprise, the monster found itself lowering its arms and hissing through his nostrils.

"Breathe…?"

"Yes, breathe deeply and lift your head."

"Hmm…" was the response.

Ivan looked on in amazement. Now this was courage! No, it was more than that, it was an example of supreme presence in the now, with great esoteric ability. To discuss meditation with a ghoul? Ivan had never seen anything like it before.

"Breathe and lift your head freely," Carl said to the monster. "With time you'll realise what your will can achieve. You don't just have to do what someone else has told you. Try to exercise will-power, the power to control your own emotions. So then, there's no use in fighting us. You're free to be yourself and do what you want. You can walk about, you can seek out quiet ponds in the depths of the forest and reflect in them, you can sing songs to the moon and build yourself a safe nest in a cave somewhere, with the soothing sound of a rustling stream outside, while owls hoot in the distance."

"Hmm, a safe nest…" the monster said dreamily. "Well, I already have that." His four arms went slack and he told them of his fenland abode, the great hut of intertwined logs and branches.

"But that's fine," Carl said. "Treasure your home, then, and appreciate the joy of having somewhere to rest your head. Be thankful for your security, your rest and calm. There is ample food in the woods for you, squirrels and hares and other things you can hunt for your survival. However, there's no need to attack us for we have an important errand. We're searching for a special rose. Perhaps you'd like to help us?"

Ivan was still listening, still sitting in the saddle like Carl, and thinking that now his commander had gone too far, recruiting monsters to their treasure hunt. He was right.

"To search for a rose? I don't have time for that and it's not really my thing. But thanks for the offer. I think I'll be slipping away to the forest's darker regions now, off to chase mice and lemmings…" He sighed with pleasure at the thought.

"Go on, then, Quriti, you do that," Carl said. "Farewell."

The huge beast turned back towards the heart of the forest, pushed away the brushwood, went into the green and disappeared. They heard him stepping on twigs and branches for a while until everything became quiet again and only birdsong and the wind rustling in the tops of the trees could be heard.

"You did a fine thing," Ivan said. "I'm impressed. No need to fight him, no, you just talked him out of it."

"Thank you," Carl said. "I'd say, always assess the situation before drawing your sword."

He went on to tell Ivan about a Japanese father who had taught his sons a lesson in this vein. The first son was called into a room; from a lintel a cat jumped down on him but the son drew his sword and spiked it. Then the second son came unwittingly into the room and was attacked by a new cat, the animal surprising him completely when it jumped on him from above. The third son was subjected to the same test, but when the cat jumped down on him it was skilfully caught in the boy's arms.

Carl concluded, "The father summed it all up for his sons. He said that the third way was the best, simply to catch the cat in your arms. You mustn't always draw your sword."

Ivan nodded and said, "Well, blimey."

Carl for his part simply winked and rode on singing, "The Grey Knight I am, I am that I am…"

Körner heard of the whole thing later, waiting back in the fenlands, when he met up with Quriti again. After the meeting with Carl, the beast had become strangely meditative and serene. Körner wasn't at all happy about how things had come to pass but the monster had at least tried and there was nothing more to be done. The hussar now released him from the service he had owed. Then Körner left the swamp and went back to the wyvern, which he mounted and flew to Nicky Woods and the Wooden Castle. Once in the forest palace, in a library of scrolls, leather-bound books and original, elegant Elzevir editions – including Galileo's *Two New Sciences* – he reported to Morven.

"So you failed again?" the monk said coldly. "Completely?"

Körner had to agree, having told him about the destruction of the metal birds and the monster's new-found emotions. After hearing the details Morven got up, left the library and took Körner along panelled corridors and passages and finally ascended a creaking spiral staircase up into the castle's highest tower.

Eventually they came to the tower chamber, a room with an arcade and a series of oak pillars through which daylight flowed.

They went out onto a balcony, sat down in wicker chairs and said nothing for a long while. Morven seemed totally lost in silent deliberations. Körner for his part looked out over the forested land, the treetops forming a carpet beneath them. He looked at the impressive peaks in the distance, their cliffs golden in the midday sun. The sky was a warm metallic blue, hazily silver as it stretched faraway.

"Just look at this," the German said at last, referring to The Land, "a view worthy of a king. And indeed you are. Here you live as a king of the forest."

"I want to be more than that," Morven said quietly.

Ringo Badger arrived with two mugs of mulled wine. They tasted the wine, old and rich, and put the mugs down on the brass table beside them.

"I can make another attempt," offered Körner. "After all, all good things come in threes, they say."

"No," said Morven simply.

"But there must be another try. The whole thing is hanging in the air at the moment."

"But not you," Morven said. "I shall personally perform the third attempt. I myself will grapple with the man, try one last trick to destroy him. I have my own methods."

"Well, you have your own crystal, don't you, so you know where he is?"

"Yes," said Morven, "I always have that with me."

Morven would get to grips with this Carl Griffensteen, and beat him with guile. Körner wasn't told what this ruse was to be, but Morven certainly had some special contacts in The Land and knew certain conditions that could ensnare Griffensteen on his way to the Rose.

CHAPTER SIX

THE CITY OF GOLD

In a serene and gently triumphant mood, Carl and Ivan rode on to seek Tiramon, the fabled City of Gold. Strengthened by their recent encounters, both good and bad, the pair now made their way through a land teeming with life, a land of resplendent greenery, blossoming flowers and flying, walking and crawling inhabitants of unknown animal kingdoms. The riders were in a mild trance, mirrored in The Land by peaceful vistas of flowers and sunshine. Eventually they rode out onto a plateau looking out over a lush, green valley, in the midst of which was situated a city, literally a shining city.

"Is it…?" asked Ivan, lost for words.

"I suppose so," Carl said.

They stopped for a while and took in the city, gleaming like gold. Actually it was indeed of gold, pure gold. Their triumphant minds had been externalised in the goal they had sought, their intentions realised. They rode down a hill into the valley and crossed a river by a bridge made of gilded wood. Before them lay Tiramon, also known as the City of Gold: its domes, roof tiles, façades and streets, everything was of gold.

According to the Book of the Worlds, which they had read in Gremoburg, here they might find the next clue to the Rose.

Approaching the city itself they passed through a neighbourhood with cherry and apple trees, banks of lupins and tulips, all made even more pleasant by the melodious chirping of many birds. The floral scent was almost intoxicating.

"Such a city, such a fabulous city," said Ivan. "It's like being in a fairy-tale."

Carl agreed that indeed this was like a tale, an instant dream, where their surroundings had the character of their realised intentions.

"Oh, I guess you're right," said Ivan, still unsure what this meant.

The pair looked somewhat out of place in this gleaming, beautiful environment. As usual, Ivan wore his grey tunic, M/16 field cap, blue-grey breeches without stripes and leather riding boots; he was armed with the sabre and the Nagant revolver and the horse he rode was brown. Carl, of course, rode a black horse with white blaze. Customarily he also wore a grey tunic, the breeches with red stripes, his boots and his uniform cap. With these he wore a scabbard belt and revolver belt. Their colours and arms didn't fit here.

Still, Carl thought, surely they were in the right place and here they would find the Rose? Was it maybe that 'The Rose That Never Fades' meant that it was made of gold, and where would you find that if not in this place?

Having passed through the gardens they rode straight into the city itself because it had neither gates nor guards. Once inside the urban area they were dazzled by all the gold but kept their composure, riding into the central square where they chanced upon a man who stood beside a tall golden façade. The man had narrow shoulders, a narrow face and well-combed dark hair in a pageboy style. His eyes were round and lively, giving him a good-natured look. He was wearing a fine jacket with gold brocade, red silk trousers with gold embroidery and boots of gilded leather.

Carl dismounted, bowed and introduced himself. "Who are you, my lord?" he continued.

"Colaxis Molumini, the Mayor of Tiramon," the man replied.

"I'm honoured," Carl said. "This is Ivan Ivanonvich, my squire."

"I see," said Colaxis, glancing up and down at their grey outfits with amused interest. Carl, however, ignored this apparent haughtiness.

"Do you know where to find The Rose That Never Fades?"

"Well, that was straight to the point, I must say!" the thin man said. "But to answer your question, yes, I do know. You must ride on to Stegion, the City of Fools. There's a wise man there who almost certainly knows it."

"A wise man in town of fools? Now I've heard everything," Carl sighed, somewhat disappointed that their journey was still not over.

"Strange, isn't it?" the mayor smiled in a friendly way. "But come along to my residence for a modest meal, since it's clear you have had a long journey."

Carl and Ivan liked the sound of this so they left their horses in servants' care and followed Colaxis to an impressive two-storey building with an elevated cornice on top of the roof, windows with alternating segmental and triangular crests and an entrance with sculpted flanks, all in gold. Inside, however, not everything was of gold after all; there was simply some gold decor in the form of gold leaf on floorboards, gold fittings on doors and frames partitioning the wall panels. Still, all the internal materials spoke of luxury: there was marble, ivory, costly wood and details in amber, mother of pearl and coral. On the walls hung tapestries with mythological scenes, depicting Streonshalk fighting the trolls, Aesir having a party in Valhalla and Odysseus meeting the sorceress Circe. The interior spoke of rest, accomplishment and fulfilment; for the moment, Carl allowed himself to indulge in that feeling, a questing soldier in need of some recreation, giving the externalising power of his mind free rein in this respect. As he was, so he saw.

In the dining hall where they finally arrived there was a violet canopy under which stood a table, laid with gold plates and goblets on a red silk cloth. They sat at the table and servants came in to serve duck stew in dill with boiled eggs as a starter dish.

"So this is the City of Gold…" Carl said dreamingly at length.

"Indeed," said the mayor. "People bring their gold here and donate it to the city, and in return they get to live here and enjoy their leisure time with good food, rest and play and study. We only have one rule here: bring your gold here but take no gold away."

"Ingenious," the knight said, appreciating the wealth of the place.

"Of course it is," Colaxis agreed. "Even you are welcome to stay here. If you can give us some gold, that is."

"That's most gracious of you, sir," Carl said, "but I don't think it's time to retire yet. No time for that since I have to find the Rose I asked you about, The Rose That Never Fades."

Next they were served deer steak with peppers and turnips.

"This is a fine meal. I am really enjoying it," said Ivan. Carl seconded this and their host bowed slightly, lowering his head almost imperceptibly in a stylish gesture, a Talleyrand of the astral world.

They finished the meal with boiled pear, ripe cheese and a dark bread, then thanked their host and went into the town. Carl for his part strolled down to the river, sat down and watched a golden barge drifting by, its deck occupied with people drinking wine and singing. Ivan sauntered off towards the city's edge, away from where they had arrived. Here he spotted a pile of silverware, just lying discarded in the sun. When a man in a gold lame suit came walking by over the fields, Ivan stopped him and asked why they had silver lying there as if thrown away. To this the man said that it was indeed discarded since they didn't value silver, only gold, for this was the City of Gold.

"So you bring out all the silver here," Ivan asked, "throwing it in this heap?"

"True, that. If anyone sometime wants to leave the City of Gold he can come here and help himself, taking all the silver that he wants."

"But why is the silver here in the first place? I mean, how does it get here if you don't value it?"

"There's no law against bringing silver here. We just don't appreciate that white metal. Call it taste, if you like. As for other expensive materials in general, yes, we do like them, like marble, oak lintels, silk, what have you. But silver? Trash, I say! Want some?"

"Later, maybe," said Ivan, bidding the man good day. He returned to the city and finally ended up by the river where Carl was lying. The captain had fallen asleep, being somewhat exhausted by their adventure and the impressions of this golden dream city, an ambiguous 'dream come true'. Now he was awakened by his squire who told him about the silver that was considered rubbish. This was excellent, thought Carl. Being pragmatic, he went back to check with Colaxis whether they could take some of the silver. The mayor agreed. He also took this opportunity to ask directions to the City of Fools, Stegion, where the 'wise man' would be, the one who knew something about the Rose.

And with that the soldiers considered themselves to be done in this place so they said goodbye to the mayor, thanked him for the meal once again, mounted their horses and rode towards the farthest approaches where they stopped to load up with some silver.

"Go for the simple things," said Carl, "like silver bullion and coins if there are any." They disputed about this for a while, since there was so much to choose from, and finally Carl made Ivan settle for one object only of each type – one goblet, one small tray and so on. Eventually all was packed into the practical Russian army issue saddlebags. Once on the road again, Ivan threw wistful glances back towards the City of Gold and its silver junk pile.

The road went away into a swampy forest, the image of the city disappeared behind a bend and they had to think ahead.

Moss and lichen hung from the trees, the air stank of putrefaction, owls hooted and a mist drifted around the trees. To ride in The Land was an odd experience; being a kind of dream land, no actual time seemed to pass and everything went by in a hazy flow. Carl didn't like this vague character of the place, he was one who demanded orderliness and transparency; so, with that thought, having intended that vision, The Land gradually became a little less blurred.

On the way to Stegion, the triumphant mood of their ride to Tiramon was disappearing, now replaced by a more neutral mindset. Carl still had a modicum of will guiding him along, however mentally he was now in a grey area and the forest they rode through mirrored that. One might say he was a man up for adventure in difficult, haunting realms and one who needed challenges; he wasn't a *bon vivant* like the Tiramon dwellers, having the sipping of sapphire wine on a golden barge as an ultimate life goal. Thus the ride through these murky woods was a logical step on the quest for the Rose.

Finally, coming out of the forest, they saw before them a dilapidated town, a complete contrast to their last arrival.

"The City of Fools, I suppose," Carl said.

"Are you sure?" asked Ivan.

The knight said nothing. Instead he rode up to the city walls, saluted the lone guard dressed in rags and gave him a silver coin. Ivan and Carl had the gate opened before them, the door halves creaking loudly as they swung up. Once inside they rode along muddy streets and saw dark houses in disrepair and some people with mad, staring eyes milling around. They rode up to a central square lined with houses that had gaudy façades and windows askew. In the centre of the square stood a bizarre, abstract sculpture consisting of disparate elements of bronze, iron, copper and wood in no apparent order. Carl absently noted the shapes; it was not a clear-cut structure, nor easy to grasp. And yet everything in The Land was of the mind, so what did this mean about his inner thoughts? The answer might be that he didn't always have the willpower to envision transparency and orderliness in every moment. Here he was a grey knight in a grey area.

They went to an inn and booked rooms for the night. Then they ventured out again to have a drink, their goal being to find the 'wise man' of Stegion who was said to know something about the legendary flower they sought. One of the buildings around the square displayed a pub sign with a picture of a jester, so they went in and looked around. It was a small, long and narrow room, surprisingly sanely decorated, adorned as it was with engraved glass in a frieze along the roof and the rest of the walls covered by varnished wood panelling.

"This is nice," said Ivan.

"Yes, but it's just a crazy town, not a ghost town or whatever."

The place was populated by lugubrious individuals wearing dark, tattered clothes, sitting at tables with cups in front of them. One of the figures stood out, however, being dressed in a green and red mi-parti tunic and a striped, pointed cap. He had a long, aquiline nose in an oblong face. It was Ringo Badger, Morven's servant, sent here at his master's bidding to ensnare the couple. Now he stood up, approached them and bowed.

"Ringo Badger, at your service, strangers. Welcome to Stegion, the City of Fools."

"Thank you."

"So then, what can I help you with? You want to know something? Do you need guidance in finding Hell or Paradise?"

"Maybe not just yet," said Carl. "But I'm fascinated by your dress, rather fancy with the red and green tunic, isn't it?"

"You like it, do you? Well, I like it myself, too, I must say. Makes me look like the model fool, fits in well here, right?"

Carl thought that maybe the man was a real fool but at least he was a friendly one. "Come and sit with us," he offered, not realising that this was the servant of Morven. Badger joined them. When each of them had a cup of beer before him, Carl asked Badger if he knew who the wisest man of this city was, since Colaxis had said that such a man in Stegion could lead them to the Rose.

"The city's wisest man…?" Badger said, pretending to think about it. "That would be Morven, I suppose. He knows the red giants and the white dwarfs, he can tame dragons and walk on fire."

"Indeed?" said Ivan. "He sounds like some obscure creature of the night."

"Well, maybe he is just that," Badger said enigmatically.

At the back of his mind, the name Morven rang a bell with Carl but for the moment he couldn't quite put his finger on it. In these strange environs, he was not thinking clearly. For his part, Morven had left his Wooden Castle in Nicky Woods and had used his crystal to know that Carl and Ivan were on their way here; so he himself had taken up residence in Stegion and had sent Badger to scout for the pair. Morven knew full well about the Rose and this quest for it, so he had informed his cronies in The Land, such as Colaxis, and thus Carl was led right to him.

"So where do we find him?" Carl asked the strange man, still not sensing the trap.

"Usually, at the cemetery at midnight," Badger said.

They finished their beer, talking for a while about other things and then they parted. Ivan and Carl waited at their lodgings until midnight and then went out and headed for the cemetery. The moon was up, ragged clouds drifted by its yellow circle and a solitary owl hooted somewhere nearby.

"This feels very weird," said Ivan. "Are you sure…?"

Carl indeed had some doubts about it all but as ever he put on a brave face.

"Cheer up now. We can't be quite sure but let's project our will onto the moment. Be the masters of circumstances, not their victims. A brave man subverts destiny and takes control of the present. At least let's try to be neutral and enjoy the fresh air."

"Thanks, mate," replied Ivan, taking a deep breath and exhaling. "Though the air isn't so fresh here in the marshes."

"I wouldn't say that," observed Carl. "I can smell refreshing soil acids."

Once at the graveyard they sat down on a granite sarcophagus. Rows of memorials faded away into the darkness; they saw tombs and crosses of iron, they saw simple wooden plates and more elaborate, carved gravestones. There was also a crypt with columns, pediments and statues on the roof.

"This looks rather precious and expensive," Ivan said, referring to the crypt.

"Oh," said Carl. "And why do you say so?"

"I mean, this is the City of Fools, everywhere we've seen is run down."

"But there are many rich fools too."

"True enough."

Just then, around the corner of this very crypt emerged an odd figure, a bald man with lips parted in an ambiguous smile, wearing a frock with a cord at the waist. Morven came right up to them, stopped and nodded gravely, introducing himself. Carl stood up and bowed.

"Delighted to meet you. Some call me the Grey Knight."

"Indeed, then it's my pleasure to meet you," Morven said and cheered inside. He had got what he wanted, having placed himself in Carl's way, that dreadful man who was serving the Light and with the power to cross all his plans. Morven sat on the sarcophagus with Carl closest to him and some moments passed in silence.

"It's good to enjoy the silence," Morven said at last.

Carl nodded. Then, perhaps because of this other-worldly setting and the presence of a 'wise man' in a timeless moment, and being a spiritual explorer, he felt the urge to talk of philosophy. A servant of the Dark, but also indeed wise, or cunning, Morven went along with this in the night-time graveyard.

"What is real?" Carl began. He still needed to find himself properly in The Land.

"Your inner mind, your spiritual self," Morven replied.

"But how does it all work here? What is the fundamental wisdom?"

"Everything is connected and still not connected."

"How should one act?"

"Do what feels right."

"How does one counter feelings of helplessness?"

"Man is helpless only if he sees himself as helpless."

"Where is this all leading?"

"There is only here and now."

"What can we do without?"

"Our sense of inferiority."

"Which is the most important distinction to make?"

"That between the conditioned and the unconditional."

"What are the most important rules of life in this place?"

"I'd say, to summon up your will, to live on the edge and to seek rest in action."

"Where is The Rose That Never Fades?"

At this sudden change of tack, the bald man raised an eyebrow. "I know that too. Come to my humble abode and I'll tell you."

CHAPTER SEVEN

MORVEN

They got up and left the graveyard, Carl and Ivan following the man along obscure, winding streets lined with bizarre buildings, eventually coming to a two-storey stone house with a yellow façade. They made their way inside and up narrow, creaking stairs, finally reaching a chamber with three ogival windows, set with stained glass plates in lead frames.

"Beautiful," Carl said, referring to the windows. "It must be a strange sight when the sun shines on them."

"Indeed so," said Morven. "The room is painted in saturated colours then." Carl looked around and noticed the tracery in the ceiling, the carved armchairs and the table set with bowls of cream morel soup. "Please do sit down," said their host and they readily obliged. How a meal could be ready on the table, as though they had been expected, was a mystery to Carl, the three of them having just met. When he pointed this out, Morven explained that Badger had helped him in the matter. They tasted the soup, enjoyed and devoured it. Then they had fried fish with steamed fennel and mashed potatoes. This was just as good. Lastly, there were pancakes with apple sauce.

"Now then," said Carl, leaning back with satisfaction when they were half-way through the pancakes, "you know something about The Rose That Never Fades. The Mayor of the City of Gold said that you would and you hinted at it yourself, in the graveyard."

"Oh yes, I'm sure I've heard a thing or two," said the monk. "I can be your guide."

Carl pondered the offer. There was something unsettling about the monk's appearance, and again that nagging suspicion at the back of his mind, that made him decide to turn it down. He didn't want this Morven as a spiritual guide in this astral realm.

"You're too kind," he replied carefully. "But I think we'll try it by ourselves. Do you have any clue as to where to look?"

"Hmm, try searching in the east. And follow your intuition," Morven advised them.

The soldiers finished their pancakes, drank a glass of cider and prepared to leave. Then Morven took out a flute from within the folds of his robe and presented it to Carl.

"Look here, take this gift," he said. "You can blow it if you get lost."

"Oh, how kind of you, thanks," said Carl, surprised. He was starting to like this monk but would still not have him as a guide. They thanked their host for the fine meal and went back to the inn, where they soon went to sleep.

In the morning sun, they mounted their horses and rode out of the City of Fools, heading east and following their intuition, as Morven had advised. They eventually reached a grassy plain and rode over it, day in and day out. It seemed to extend indefinitely in all directions. There wasn't a hill, nor a grove of trees, nothing, just miles and miles of steppe like a green ocean. They were in a no-man's-land, a psychological landscape that spoke of barrenness, monotony and disorientation.

Riding a little ahead, Carl squinted against the sun, reined in his horse as he waited for Ivan and suggested a break. They dismounted and Ivan began to make a fire with his tinderbox as Carl just sat and watched, being exhausted. Soon the crackling of the fire was heard, a pot came out and Ivan warmed some wine. Before long, their spirits began to rise.

"The sun's high," observed Ivan, but Carl didn't react. "This plain gives me the jitters. When will we arrive? It feels as if we're approaching the edge of the world. Still, the Earth's round, isn't it?"

"But this isn't Earth, this is The Land."

Ivan put another stick on the fire and ducked from the sparks. "Some of my villagers back home still think the Earth is flat," he muttered.

"What's the name of the village?"

"Gerasina, south of Tula."

"Ah, if only we were in our normal world," Carl sighed. "The everyday world with countries like Finland and Sweden, Russia and Germany. But now we're in a parallel world, a fairy-tale world where the landscape is a projection of our inner minds. I'm getting tired of this!"

"You are?" said Ivan, surprised. "You want to return to that everyday world, even though there's a war going on there? Even though you haven't finished the glorious quest we're on?"

"Yeah," Carl said. "Sort of." It was not so easy navigating The Land. They'd been sent here and there and now they were nowhere.

"There's a saying I once heard: be careful what you wish for, you might get it."

Carl nodded at the wisdom of this; it was especially true in this world, The Land literally being made up of one's dreams and intentions. He understood that if only he could start to think positively then the landscape would change according to his mind, become a place of opportunities instead of a depressing sight as now. "As we are, we see," the wise man had said. But for the moment he just lacked the willpower to steer his mind along those lines and just stared listlessly out over the plain. However, he stopped himself from wishing them back in the normal world, the world of 1917 where a world war was raging. 'In The Land I am and here I'll remain until I'm done,' he told himself. *J'y suis, j'y reste*, as General MacMahon had said at Malakoff.

Carl looked absently out across the plain and suddenly, on the horizon, as if in response to his determination this very moment, he spotted something. From the east, two riders were approaching. Carl pointed them out to Ivan and they both waited in silence, hands on holsters, until the two newcomers arrived.

Over the grasses two diminutive men on two equally diminutive horses now approached. One of the men wore armour made of lacquered leather, wooden plates and iron scales; on his head was a helmet with wings and in his scabbard was a curved sword. Under the armour he seemed to be wearing a chemise and breeches of silk. All the details of the clothing, armour and weapons were exquisitely worked. The rider's countenance was neutral, slightly grim, and his dark, narrow eyes betrayed no emotion. His companion was a gentler figure with a bamboo hat on his head, armour of bamboo plates and in his belt he carried a sword without a scabbard. He wore a black cotton dress.

"Good afternoon, gentlemen," the more elaborately dressed of the newcomers said.

"Good afternoon," Carl replied. "So you speak our language although you clearly come from a distant land?"

"Yes, we do. But this is not the normal world, is it?" said the newcomer. "This is The Land, a world of thought."

"Indeed," Carl said, realising that he should have known better, "the dream world of everyone." Making a welcoming gesture he bade the pair sit down and have some wine with them.

The two Japanese got off their horses and produced their own porcelain cups; they were served by Ivan who also gave his master and himself some more.

The samurai took a sip of the warm drink and whatever he

thought about it he betrayed no emotion, just nodded. He introduced himself as Yoritomo, his companion Shensi. They had
come from the 15th century, when it had become possible for the
Japanese to go abroad as merchants and mercenaries, and the two
had been travelling in China for a while. In the Middle Kingdom
they had been enlisted by a prince who was planning to overthrow
a rival feudal lord. But in the aftermath of this war, Yoritomo had
been approached by a *bodhisattva* who had given him a great mission: to find a particular cup that the Buddha himself was said to
have used, and to perform this quest as a spiritually enlightening
endeavour for the East. And since Yoritomo liked challenges, he
had undertaken the mission without hesitation, not even seeking
any expenses since chivalry was not only a Western virtue.

So Yoritomo took Shensi with him to find the Buddha's Teacup.
By now they had been searching for it quite some time, in China,
India and Nepal before finding their way into The Land, the enigmatic astral world where Carl and Ivan also rode, equally without
much success in their adventure. Yoritomo had begun to experience a certain hopelessness and despair too.

"Brother!" cried Carl. "We're also on a seemingly hopeless
quest." He told the Japanese about the mission given to him by
an angel of God to find The Rose That Never Fades – and what
the errant paths in this fairy-tale world had led to. When he had
finished talking, no-one said anything for a long while.

"But wait," Ivan said eventually, "I think I have an idea…"
The others eyed him incredulously. "Let's change missions – for
a time." Carl and Yoritomo both raised an eyebrow at the same
time. Ivan continued, "You two carry out our mission for a while
and see if you have any luck, and we'll do yours. It might give us a
fresh view on it all, seeing things the others haven't seen."

"How about the language problem, then?" said Yoritomo.

"We can talk to each other here, can't we?"

"But I mean, if we fall back into the normal world again,"

said the samurai, "which sometimes happens to us, what do we do then?"

"Hmm…" said Ivan, deep in thought, and then got a new idea. "I'll come with you and Shensi can accompany Carl! And should we stumble back into the ordinary world we'll be guaranteed to have an interpreter!"

"Well, hmm, no," said Carl. "I mean, we can certainly talk to each other here. But if Shensi and I ended up in China, we couldn't talk to each other then, could we?"

"Well, no, you're right," said Ivan, thinking some more. He was determined to get his idea working. "But we can communicate here and that's a start. Once in the ordinary world, should we chance to end up there, we'll have to communicate with hired interpreters or sign language. We know, after all, what our missions are, our respective tasks. Then we'll just have to try and find our way back to The Land."

"Your proposal is interesting," said Yoritomo. "I'd say we should strike a deal. Nothing could be worse than it already is."

"Exactly my opinion," said Carl and put down his cup. "Our search for the Rose has reached a dead end so I welcome any new ideas. Even to do something else for a while, like searching for – what was it called – the Buddha's Teacup? Good thinking, Ivan. I knew I'd chosen a fine man!"

They sealed the deal by shaking hands, promising each other to meet here again when they felt the time was right. In this land of the mind, they would simply intend it. So now they broke camp and went off in new directions, Carl to the east with Shensi to look for Buddha's Teacup and Ivan with Yoritomo to the west in search of the Rose.

Carl and Shensi began their quest with renewed energy. Eventually a peasant they chanced upon told them of a certain hermit who could give them a clue in their search for the cup. To reach the man they rode along a path between plane trees, bamboo and hazel, soon coming to a steep mountain where they had to dismount.

"Indeed some strange mountains they have here," Carl said, "steep and conical."

"But this is how things look in our fairy-tales," said Shensi. "This is my kind of fairy world, the kind of Chinese-flavoured world that I had narrated to me as a child."

"Aha," said Carl, "so we find ourselves in your projections now. And this is because I'm playing along with you and I'm currently seeking the Buddha's Teacup… A new experience for my mind!"

Shensi nodded, adding, "The hermit should live in a cave nearby so we'll just go on slowly for a while, on foot."

Leading the horses, they continued along the narrow trail. They could hear cawing birds and the roar of a stream that rushed down a mountain; soon they could see it from the trail, too, the water racing along and over edges and falling straight down into a large pool. Illuminated by the sun, the rising, vaporised droplets formed a rainbow.

Carl watched his new friend in the straw hat, black pyjamas and bamboo armour, going before him leading his little horse. How strange, the knight thought, that apart from the somatic differences he was a lot like old Ivan, carefree, resourceful and positive. It was hard to imagine that he would end up in an adventure with this Japanese fellow, like Carl out on a ride in the astral world yet for the moment with a Russian as companion instead of his usual master. It also made him wonder what Yoritomo and Ivan could be experiencing right now.

Eventually Shensi spotted a cave in the mountainside. They left the horses on a ledge, tied to a tree, and set off along an even narrower path. It wound its way treacherously up the steep mountainside; at one point they even had to push themselves flat against the rock, turning their feet in line to keep their footing. Soon, however, they had reached the entrance of the cave. Shensi took off his straw hat and Carl his Russian uniform cap, in respect.

"I'd be glad if you could talk to the hermit," Carl said, not having the inspiration to lead and take charge just now, even though he was an army officer.

"I'd be glad too, but..." Shensi was also hesitating.

"You're a little more at home here."

"I might be, sir," Shensi said, "but this is a fairy-tale world even for me. I wasn't born in The Land, I was born in Japan."

They went into the cave. The walls were damp and there were puddles on the floor. First the passageway darkened but soon they came to an open space, a hall illuminated by a light shaft. There was no sign of life here so with Shensi in the lead they ventured forth into another tunnel. After a bend they came out into another hall, this one illuminated by enigmatic emeralds in the stone walls. On a rocky podium a man sat and meditated, a mysterious monk in a cotton kaftan and with a liberated, spiritual countenance. Shensi and Carl both knelt down and remained like this for a few minutes. Then the Japanese dared to lift his head.

"Master, we are Shensi and Carl Griffensteen. We are honoured to be in your presence for here one can undeniably feel that the vast Nothingness is ever-present." The monk nodded, barely visibly, so Shensi continued. "May you live in eternal harmony, master. It's like this – we are on a mission to find the Buddha's Teacup. Can you give us any clue as to where to find it?"

Water dripped into a puddle. The emeralds sparkled. Water continued to drip and the hermit replied with an eloquent silence for what seemed an eternity.

"Certainly, I know about that cup," he said quietly at last. "Ask the monkey and you might find it."

"Who is the monkey? Where...?"

"I've given my answer. Now I must go into *pancatva*. Farewell."

At that very moment, the figure before them dissolved into a bright, crystalline fog, the five elements of which we all consist returning to wind, water, earth, fire and ether. All that remained was the man's cowl, neatly folded in a pile where he had been sitting.

"What in the world…?" Carl exclaimed. But Shensi just nodded and remained silent.

CHAPTER EIGHT

THE BIRD

The emerald light of the cave shone onto the podium and its cowl, the only remnant of the deceased hermit. With reverence, the Japanese backed out of the hall, the soldier following his example. Once back in the area with the light shaft, they turned and walked out of the cave. After an equally nerve-wracking passage along the narrow ledge, they reached their horses on the path. Carl wondered silently why it was that every time he seemed to be getting somewhere the way disappeared.

"So what did the hermit mean," Carl said, "about asking a monkey?"

"Well," said Shensi, "I once heard a story about a humanoid ape, an Ape King, but that was a long time ago. We'll have to find someone who knows where he lives."

In the no-time of The Land, they then rode from place to place, trying to solve the riddle of who the monkey was. They asked kings and queens, wise men and fools, merchants and swordsmen if they knew who this Ape King was. They sought the answer in a gilded wooden temple hidden in the pine forest, in a magnificent palace on top of a mountain and in a small pagoda beside a pond where coloured fish swam. They travelled a trade route, talking with merchants who sold myrrh, frankincense and asphalt, and they bought information from proud warriors in lacquered leather armour and helmets, decked with giant birds' beaks and antlers. No-one, however, was able to give them any clue. Most simply laughed.

Yet finally, from a tavern host they learned that the Ape King was real and lived on the Flower and Fruit Mountain. Carl gave the man a silver coin. Having refreshed themselves with some rice wine the pair continued their ride and after some time came to a lush forest where birds sang and monkeys chattered; these creatures swung between branches, sat eating bananas or played together in the grass. There was every kind from proboscis monkeys and mandrills to chimpanzees, baboons and gibbons. The whole neighbourhood was strewn with flowers, red and blue and bright yellow, and the trees were hung with fruit of all kinds. Shensi reached up his hand and grabbed a banana from a bunch, took the fruit, peeled and ate it contentedly.

"Could we be near the Flower and Fruit Mountain?" he said between mouthfuls. Carl peered about, glimpsed a mountain between the trees and nodded.

"Probably," he said. "Now we just have to find the special monkey, the king himself."

They rode up to the foot of the mountain and marvelled at the undulating, looming shapes of the cliff covered with flowers and trees. Not least, they sensed intoxicating, fragrant scents. Some apes approached them watchfully, in the lead a powerful gorilla who stood up on his hind legs and asked who they were. When the formalities were completed, the tribe relaxed and became friendly and curious.

"Where is your king?" asked Shensi eventually. "We have come far to find him." At this the gorilla became sad.

"Oh, what misfortune! During a sojourn at the palace of the King of Heaven once, he became angry at some insult and went berserk. He was severely punished for this so now he is forced to dwell in a hidden rocky cell with the Buddha's seal on it. He won't get out of there for a long time."

"Well, I'll be damned," Carl said aside to Shensi. "After so much effort, another dead end. So what do we do now?"

"Cheer up, sir," the other said philosophically. "We have, after all, found out something valuable, that the Ape King could hold a clue to the whereabouts of the Teacup. But we'll need help to learn any more. It may be time to return to the plain and see what Yoritomo and Ivan have found out during their search."

"Indeed," said Carl. "You're a wise fellow. Now it feels right to return to the plain."

They exchanged gifts with the monkeys, giving them some glass beads and receiving a large basket of fruit. Then they rode back to the plain.

Strangely, it was not hard to find Yoritomo and Ivan who, during their quest in the western fairy-tale world, had found out one thing.

"What's that, then?" asked Carl as they sat by a fire and drank mulled wine, surrounded by the desolate landscape.

"We can get the answer in a city floating in the eternal ether," said Ivan triumphantly.

"Come again?"

"There's a floating city called Ghislane where there are answers to many things, so they say."

Carl contemplated this information for a while. Then he informed Yoritomo on the outcome of the eastern quest, that the Ape King had the answer although he himself was imprisoned in a distant mountain now. Having wished each other well they agreed to part, the east-west brotherhood being dissolved. Thus they had helped each other in their respective missions and now they would continue as before, going their separate ways. This friendship, however, had great value beyond this day and would prove very useful for Carl and Ivan later in their adventure.

Carl and Ivan rode back towards the west but they found neither the floating city nor the Rose nor even anyone to ask. They rode on through another endless forest until stopping by a clearing next to a creek. Carl looked up at the clouds in the sky. He rubbed his forehead, grimaced and wondered what to do; it was like being on the steppe again, lost and without clues. Ivan suggested that they dismount so they did so and the Russian led the horses down to a stream for a drink. Carl also then went down to the river, drank from the fresh water and filled his bottle, corked it and sat down on a tree stump to relax.

He meditated for a while, letting the babbling waters and the birdsong calm him down. Soon he barely even heard these pastoral sounds, instead he shut everything out, not even hearing the sound of his own breathing. Peace, I am, peace, I am…

At length he came out of his trance. An evening sun was shining on his face and it felt like time to sleep. How long had he meditated? He didn't know. The neighing of the horses nearby assured him that they were still safely there. A popping sound behind him sounded like a bonfire, and indeed it was for when he turned around he saw that the faithful Ivan had made a fire and was about to prepare a bird for grilling. Carl stood up, went to the fire, took a little mulled wine in a beaker and breathed out slowly.

"So what are we to do?" Ivan asked. "Should we sleep on it? Lost we are, that's for sure."

"Lost on a wide, wide sea," said Carl. Yet now it somehow didn't feel quite so desolate.

They waited for the burning wood to turn into glowing embers, Carl smoking his pipe the while, enjoying the sweet flavour of *Gävle Vapen*. Then they grilled the grouse. They ate, drank wine and rested, and they even fell asleep. They didn't bother to take turns in guarding the camp, they just slept; whoever wanted to sneak up on them and kill them was welcome to try, Carl thought. It was fate. After all, they had trusted to it during the whole sojourn in The Land.

Carl awoke again to sunshine, looked up into an endless sky and then he knew what to do. He sat up and looked in the bags for something edible, finding a dark piece of bread and some fruit given by the monkeys; he mixed a little fresh water with wine in a cup, sat down on a log and ate. Once Ivan had also awoken and had something to eat, Carl took out the flute given to him by Morven, showing it to Ivan.

"Aah, that's the solution!" said the squire. "Morven said we could blow that pipe if we got lost. I'd forgotten about that."

"Indeed, so had I," said Carl. He still had his suspicions about the strange monk, but his mind was calmer and stronger now. Moreover, they had little choice, so he blew a note.

Nothing happened, not at first. But soon there appeared in the skies a circling bird, a creature with feathers of soot and beak of orange, a large blackbird. It flew in to land on Carl's sleeve and nodded a greeting.

"What's the word?" said the bird.

"What's the word?" Carl repeated. "Well, we're lost and need some guidance. That's the word."

"Guidance, hmm…" repeated the bird mysteriously, its head on one side.

"A man named Morven gave me this flute to blow if we got lost," explained Carl, "and now we want to be led."

"Where to?"

"To The Rose That Never Fades."

"I do not know what that is. But I can show you to Morven's palace."

"Back in the City of Fools?"

"No, he doesn't live there, he's got a veritable palace in a mysterious forest, Nicky Woods. The palace itself is called the Wooden Castle since it's made entirely of wood, a towering structure of grotesque beauty. That's where he resides."

Carl was still wary of Morven. But in the current state of affairs, lacking clues, he was glad of any help they could get even if it meant he would be beholden to that man. Carl's mind would just have to be the stronger.

Therefore, Carl and Ivan broke camp, mounted their horses and rode away following the little bird as it flew in front of them through copses of deciduous trees arching overhead, across meadows of white flowers and finally through a woodland of hoary, ancient trees. These trees were unfathomably tall, pine and spruce and the occasional birch, and the path they followed was tortuous and bumpy. They could barely see anything ahead but the blackbird nevertheless still led the way, flying in circles above their heads and urging them on.

After who could know how long, they came to a road in the forest, a man-made passage paved with smooth granite blocks. They followed this path as the bird flew along it, and at last they came to the Wooden Castle, the multi-storey palace with roof overhangs, crannies and balconies, supported by tarred fir pillars and decorated with skilful ornamentation in an ageless, rustic fashion. Shingle covered the roofs, the windows had lead-lined panes and red shutters and the door was made of smooth, varnished oak.

"Thank you, blackbird," Carl said to the creature when it landed on his sleeve again. "I guess this is Morven's palace, then."

"This is it," said the bird. "So I guess I'm free now? You have what you wanted?"

"Indeed. Thank you kindly, wonderful bird."

"Free, I'm free!" chirped the pathfinder bird and rose into the high heavens, striking up a song and was gone.

Carl and Ivan now found themselves in a dim, old forest, sitting on horseback in front of a Wooden Castle that lost itself in the heights of the trees with its intricate, rustic architecture adorned with carved figures, floral ornamentation and animal symbols. They dismounted and left their horses untied in the dark forecourt of the palace, the animals soon finding their way down to a creek where they quenched their thirst after the long journey. Everything was shadowed in this forest, the tall trees intertwining their branches and shutting out the presence of light. Carl went up the front porch stairs, approached the door and let the heavy knocker fall. Soon someone arrived and opened a small hatch in the door.

"What do you want?" said Ringo Badger, dressed in his customary conical, striped woollen cap.

"Oh, it's you," said Carl, surprised. "We met in the City of Fools."

"It sure is me," said Badger, brightening up. "And now I see that you're Carl Griffensteen and you have your squire Ivan Ivanovich along. Come in, come in, by all means."

The hatch was closed, the door opened and the pair were led into the entrance hall with its bearskins and hunting weapons on the walls, then further along corridors and galleries and through chambers and hallways lined with doors to unknown rooms. Finally they began to hear music, bizarre music produced by the bellows and pipes of a harmonium. They were led into a large room with high-beamed ceilings, Persian rugs, and tables and shelves adorned with strange *objets d'art*. At the furthest end of the hall they saw an instrument with carved pipes in the shape of animal heads, the whole arrangement so high that the player himself was invisible.

Badger ventured before them and ended up standing discreetly by the side of the organ, trying to catch the attention of the performer. While he was doing this, Ivan and Carl enjoyed the sad but beautiful tones, the strange cadences that talked of the forest's solitude, the beauty of the twilight and the melancholy world of passion and power. Eventually the music stopped and a bald man emerged from behind the instrument. Morven was, as usual, dressed in a dark kaftan. He immediately noticed the two soldiers and smiled his thin smile.

"Aah, the Grey Knight, as it were. We meet again."

"Indeed we do. We became a little lost so I blew the whistle."

"The flute," said Morven knowingly, "and my little bird brought you here. How fortuitous."

"So now we need your help, to know the way to the Rose, a better way. The eastern road we travelled was in vain. Maybe we did make good friends there in the east but now I'm lost for ideas. Can you be our guide, please?"

Carl had bitten the bullet. He actually didn't want Morven as a guide, having already turned down his offer once before. But now they seemed to have no other choice but to rely on Morven's counsel, sink or swim. The man gave Carl a strange feeling and he didn't trust him, but then one can't let personal chemistry get in the way when the fate of the world is at stake. And with that thought about relationship, he suddenly remembered where he'd heard the monk's name before: he was the somewhat estranged husband of the enigmatic lady, Parysatis. The captain began to realise that some greater plan had been afoot all along, but he kept his thoughts to himself for now.

"I think I can help you," said Morven, delighted to have ensnared the awful fellow at last. "How can I say no to a little ride through these impossible climes? But first, something to eat!" He clapped his hands and Badger nodded and left them.

They went to a salon with pine panelling, bottle glass windows and a table with elaborate chairs. First they had a glass of vodka with wild lingonberry juice. Then came other servants with marinated fillet of bear, hare stew, roast swan with forest turnips and finally a rustic cheesecake with blueberry jam. With all this they drank beer and red juice.

"So you're really a forester?" observed Carl as they ate dessert. "You're not at home in the City of Fools?"

"Oh, I live here and there," said Morven, enigmatic as ever. "I thrive in shady neighbourhoods, you could say, not specifically beside the graveyards of crazy towns."

The fine meal finished, Morven produced a zither and played them a curious tune, a series of half-tone shifts and wavering sounds in a hypnotic rhythm. Then Carl and Ivan were taken to their respective chambers, Carl's having its own fireplace with hot embers on the hearth. His stomach well satisfied, despite there being no need whatever for food in The Land, and his mind settled, he plunged into a bed of eider down bolsters and slept before his head hit the pillow.

CHAPTER NINE

SLANKA

The next day they breakfasted on flatbread, salted herring and beer. Then they immediately took off, the three of them venturing out towards the place where, hopefully, the Rose would be. Morven, the man professing to show the way, was now dressed in riding boots, breeches of black silk, a tunic of red cloth, a cocked hat and a short cloak, his usual kaftan having now been discarded as unsuitable for riding. During the ride, Morven informed the others that the Rose could be searched for on a mysterious island surrounded by a circular river. The island was named Slanka, and there they would seek out a place called Sunnyglade. There the Rose was said to live. They rode through the woodland until they caught sight of light between the trees, a bright, orange light.

"Light," exclaimed Ivan, "that was strange."

"But not just light," said Carl, "it's hot too! Is it a forest fire?"

"Wait and see," said Morven mysteriously. "Let's ride closer."

Approaching the place they heard the roar of flames and soon saw what it was all about: a burning river. Sharp flames rose from the water and spread their heat, reaching for the sky and turning into smoke. Something like this they had never seen before.

"I know what this is," said Morven and turned his face away from the heat. "This is Ladolios, a river one must cross to get to the Rose."

"But how?" wondered Carl.

"Ladolios is a circular river, a river that runs round and round forever, and the other side is the island of Slanka. There, in Sunnyglade, grows The Rose That Never Fades. But how to get across, not even I know."

Carl now began to suspect a trick, for Morven must have known about this all along and had given them no hint of the difficulty to be faced. But his meditation the previous day, followed by good sleep, had calmed his mind and he was ready for anything. They rode back into the woods a bit to escape the worst of the heat, then rode parallel to the river to see if there were any bridge or ford or the like. After an hour's ride, the sharp-eyed Ivan pointed to an object on the riverbank.

"Look there! A boat!"

"And not only that," said Carl when he caught sight of it too, "there's a man next to the boat!"

"Indeed," said Morven, "it's a waterman."

In fact, Morven knew perfectly well that this waterman was there, waiting in his boat. So he now urged his horse on to get to the ferryman quickly and strike a deal with him. But the alert Carl followed by Ivan beat him to it by their superior horsemanship, riding on past Morven and reaching the beach quickly. Once there, in the vicinity of the boatman, they dismounted and walked bravely on, not allowing themselves to be troubled by the heat from the river.

Morven's horse riding skills had not been honed, like the others', by three years of war so he lagged behind, cursing this fact that effectively scuppered his plans. His plan had been to make sure that Carl never left this neighbourhood, trapped forever, and he had intended to bribe the ferryman to leave the oar to Carl. Thereby Carl would himself have become the boatman, serving on the fiery river for eternity. However, Morven now didn't have time to do this, for as he rode in the wake of the soldiers they had already started to negotiate with the man, named Thonon, about crossing the river, offering him some of their silver. Thonon was an old, strip-bearded, hollow-cheeked man with sad eyes.

"Sure, I can take you over," he said. "But I have no use for silver."

"But how come your boat isn't melting or burning up? And how can you yourself handle the heat so well?" Carl asked incredulously.

"Well, you tell me... Are you in or out?"

"Yes, of course we're in," said Carl. "Let's do it." He led his horse towards the boat and Ivan followed. Once at the shoreline Carl suddenly hesitated, not only because of the heat but wondering whether the boat could really carry two men with their horses.

"Come on, jump in! With horses and everything," Thonon said. "Two horses I can take. But not three."

So the captain got aboard the boat with his horse and all, duly followed by his squire. The small craft was now completely full and low in the water, while the heat from the burning river was excruciating too. "Warm and comfortable," observed Carl, keeping a straight face.

"Indeed it is," Thonon said drily and began to push the boat away from the shore with his oar. They then saw Morven finally arriving at the beach.

"The boat could only take two horses!" cried Ivan. Morven tried to put on a brave face and waved.

"Good luck, then. I'll be waiting here."

Morven was angry about this development, not having had the time to bring Thonon into his plans. So what would he do now? He couldn't tell Thonon to return after the crossing since that would seem suspicious; he couldn't show any personal interest in the Rose. He couldn't even cry out to the boatman after the travellers had disembarked on the other side because the river was too wide for this.

Expertly, Thonon brought his passengers over the river, whose flames seemed to swerve around the boat so that the heat was actually bearable aboard, Carl noticed. However, he could see the suffering of the ferryman whose expression bore traces of deep sorrow. What debt was he paying off by serving at this hellish river? The waters were about two miles wide, a considerable distance which they travelled for about an hour. When they reached the shore of the island, the legendary Slanka, the pair got off with their horses.

"So what would you like for payment?" the knight asked Thonon.

"I have no use for gold or silver or things like that," the man said. "But maybe you could find some way to help me out of my predicament. As punishment for taking a harp belonging to a deva, I was made to come here a long, long time ago. This is my punishment, being waterman at Ladolios until the very end of time."

"So that's why you're so sad," said Carl.

"Yes. Imagine for yourself to be kept on this burning river, day in and day out, carrying people to and from the island."

"So you want us to help get you out of here?" The ferryman nodded. "I'll think about it," Carl said, "I promise. We'll be back soon."

They bade farewell and rode into the country before them, the mysterious island of Slanka surrounded by the burning river Ladolios. They didn't have Morven as a guide anymore but that didn't matter since they could look for inhabitants of the place to ask the way to Sunnyglade, the abode of the Rose. They rode through a forest of pine and birch, a wagtail singing in a tree above.

"Is this Hell?" asked Ivan.

"What makes you think that?"

"The burning river, the boatman…"

"Well, good point. But no, I don't think so," said Carl, guessing. His mind didn't feel troubled, as it surely would be in Hell. "This is just Slanka, a land surrounded by a somewhat fiery river. If we're lucky we can complete the first part of our mission here."

Along the trail they came to a village, a collection of farmhouses either side of a cobbled street. It was apparently a prosperous place; all the houses were tarred and had ornamented shutters, green doors and shingled roofs. However, the villagers themselves that the riders came across seemed sad.

"Why are you so troubled?" Carl asked a man in a slouch hat and homespun tunic.

"Our apple trees don't bear fruit anymore." He pointed to a tree in the village centre, perfectly bare and withered.

"I don't know what to say about that," Carl replied. "But maybe I'll think of something later. I might return. We'll see."

He asked the way to Sunnyglade and was told to keep on the same path. And so they rode on and eventually came to a town with half-timbered houses, broad streets and a well in the town square. But here, too, the people they met were sad.

"Our well has run dry. What should we do?" a fat man in a beret, cape and breeches said when questioned. The riders approached and looked down into the well shaft, seeing that the bottom consisted only of bare, dry stones. Carl shook his head.

"I don't know what to do about this," he said again. "But I'll ponder the problem and maybe I'll think of something. I'll return soon."

Carl Griffensteen had no answers for the three curses. But he thought that they might well come to him soon, since everything was going his way now. Again they had been told to stay on the same path so they rode on in silence for a while and eventually came to a copse, a gathering of deciduous trees. Suddenly, on the right-hand side of the way, they saw a wooden sign on a pole. They rode closer and Carl bent down to read it.

"'Follow this path to get to Sunnyglade' it says. Sunnyglade! But that's exactly what we're looking for! Morven told us that the Rose is there. And here it is, the sign we need!"

"Sometimes you're just lucky," said Ivan.

"Lucky, perhaps," said Carl. "But we've come a long way to find this place." He threw his leg over the horse's withers and jumped to the ground. "My good friend," he said to his squire, "I'd better do this alone since I was given the mission."

"As you wish, sir," agreed Ivan, dismounting and lying down on a bed of moss beside the road. The horses went off to nibble at the flowers. Carl rubbed his hands, breathed out, took another deep breath and embarked on the path to Sunnyglade. At last, he thought, my search for this Rose, this shimmering legend, is nearing its end.

He followed the path into mysterious, peaceful woods and felt as though he didn't have a problem in the world. At a certain point, he rounded a bend in the trail and came out into a clearing. In the middle of it he saw something that glittered. He walked slowly up to it, bent down and saw that it was indeed a golden rose, shining like the sun. He touched it; it was soft like a living plant but the very lustre was not to be mistaken. It was gold. Now this wasn't junk silver as in Tiramon. But then Carl suffered a moment's hesitation: what should he do now? Was he really going to pick this beautiful plant? Would that not be sacrilege, to kill it? But then he heard a small voice.

"Pick me!"

"What?"

"You heard me," said the Rose, for it was indeed the plant speaking, "pick me! You've searched for me far and wide and now you've found me!"

"Aah… you can talk!"

"Yes, of course I can. I'm not stupid," said the flower. "And I also have an inkling that you have some questions on your mind. So, my friend, take this opportunity and pose them now because once you've picked me I shall no longer be able to speak, of course."

"Fine, and you're right," Carl said, and thought of the troubles he had encountered on the way here. "Well, firstly I passed a village with apple trees that didn't bear fruit. Do you know what the problem is?"

The Rose immediately had the answer. "Oh, that? It's like this — mice burrow down and gnaw at the roots. Kill the mouse beneath one tree, then all the trees should start giving apples again."

"Really? Thank you, the villagers will be pleased. But then I came to a town with a dried-up well. What's the problem there?"

"Aha, that well again, eh? I'd say that under a stone at the foot of the well lives a toad. Kill the toad and the well will start flowing with water again."

"Thank you again," said Carl. "Now, there's one final big problem. There was a boatman..." He told the Rose about Thonon's unhappy life. The flower even had a solution to this dilemma and told Carl all about it.

"I am deeply grateful to you," said the soldier, "and so will many others be. Now should I pick you?"

"Lovely, go on and do it," said the Rose.

Carl took out his sharp Russian army knife and cut the stem carefully, took the Rose and held it up to the sun, admiring its lustre. And in that moment something strange happened: where the Rose had grown a new, identical flower sprouted up, as beautiful and as golden as the first.

"How strange," Carl said to himself. "It seems as though a golden rose should always grow here. Creation isn't complete without it, as it were."

"That is so," said the new rose. "There must always be a rose here, as an object of dreams. Of everybody's dreams, for they should never die."

"I see," said Carl. "So farewell, flowering golden rose in the glade. May you be the goal of another adventurer, and prosper here forever and ever, inspiring men to dream." He tucked the rose he had picked into an inside pocket of his grey tunic and walked back along the trail.

"Did you find it?" Ivan asked when again they met. Carl nodded.

"Yes, I have found The Rose That Never Fades. After all our searching across The Land, I have it in my pocket." He produced the flower and showed it to his friend who marvelled greatly at it. Carl put the flower safely back inside his tunic. "But let us now return across this island. Then, when we've crossed the fiery river, we'll ride to the Flowery Meadow and meet Pelagion to find out what we need this most expensive Rose for!"

"What's this Flowery Meadow, then?" asked Ivan.

"Our next destination," said Carl. "When I met the angel Pelagion in Castle Munte, he said that I should go there when I'd found the Rose."

The pair mounted and rode away in the gentle sunshine, back along the path. Soon they came to the town where the well had run dry. Carl, remembering what the Rose had said, rode straight into the square and called the fat man in the beret over to him.

"I have the solution to your worries. Under a stone at the foot of the well lives a large toad. If you kill the toad, the well will provide water again." The man immediately called others to help and arranged for some ropes to let down a slim and brave, armed man to the bottom of the well. Once down there the fellow examined the rocks, found the toad and killed it with a single rapier thrust. That very moment the water began to flow and the man was hoisted up. All the townspeople flocked around and could soon see that the well yielded water again; they cheered for Carl and Ivan, waving them goodbye since they wanted to be on their way again.

Soon they came to the village with the withered trees.

"The answer to the problem," Carl told the man in the slouch hat, "is that mice are gnawing at the roots. Just kill the mouse beneath the one tree in the centre here and all the trees should also start to produce fruit again." The man brought up others with shovels who began to dig around the tree's roots. Soon they found the wily mouse and killed it with a blow of a shovel. At that moment the tree's branches started to become green again and yielded beautiful ripe apples. The man in the slouch hat picked two.

"Please," he said to Carl and Ivan, "take these as thanks!"

"Thank you, yeoman. But now we have to continue on our way."

He put the red, shiny apple in his other inside pocket and rode on towards Ladolios, the fiery river, while Ivan ate his fruit on the go. Once at the river bank they met Thonon, the ferryman, waiting with his boat.

"Good day, sirs. I hope your journey has been successful. Well, do you have an answer to my dilemma?"

"I do," said Carl. "Have no fear. Take us over and then I'll tell you."

Thonon received the two adventurers and their horses, rowing them over the fiery stream in his iron boat. Once on the other side and safely on terra firma, Carl told the man what Morven had known all along.

"When you meet the next man that comes along, wanting to cross the river, let him into your boat and give an oar to him. When he accepts it you can jump ashore and leave this place for good!"

"Thank you, that's a response I'd say sounds good enough," said Thonon. "Soon I'll be free! God bless you!"

"No, you can thank God and the Rose," Carl said, patting his tunic pocket. Neither man was concerned that some other unfortunate was to be tricked into the eternal task of crossing among the flames. It would be fate.

Carl mounted his horse and rode off with his companion. Shortly after this they found Morven, taking a nap beneath an oak a safe distance away from the burning river. Carl got down, walked up to him and tugged at his robes. The bald monk opened his eyes sleepily.

"W…what? W…who?" he exclaimed.

"It is us, Carl and Ivan."

"Aha. Right, so I see."

Morven seemed bleak, almost shocked to see his enemy back here. He had thought to imprison Carl as boatman on the river of fire, but the warrior of Light had been way ahead of him, leaving Morven behind, foiled. But he recovered his composure and kept a stoic straight face, just smiling his mocking smile.

"So, did you find the Rose?"

"Yes, I did," said Carl, patting himself on the pocket.

Immediately Morven wanted to take the Rose away from Carl and throw it into some dark abyss, or maybe the fiery river itself. But he couldn't. He wasn't a man of action like that, not trained as a soldier, and if he tried to wrestle with Carl and failed he would lose face. Moreover, the man had a squire to back him up. Morven may alternatively have been schooled in dark arts but neither could he exert actual magic in the presence of this knight in broad daylight; Carl's aura was too strong for that kind of thing to work, the man being the epitome of will and courage. Thinking fast, the monk certainly had other plans though.

"Then I guess we'll part here," was all he said.

"I guess so," Carl said.

There was no farewell, for Morven could barely conceal his hostility. He was after all in the service of the Dark, a sworn enemy to Carl and his mission, and he had been beaten here. He simply mounted his horse and rode off to the west.

"Odd chap," said Ivan. "He suddenly seemed so angry."

"Indeed," was all that Carl said on the matter. But he was beginning to understand Morven's real nature as their enemy. "But let's ride off ourselves," he continued, "to the Flowery Meadow and to meet up with the angel Pelagion."

CHAPTER TEN

THE ARMY OF THE DARK

Morven rode to the west, using the mysterious mental confluences of The Land to summon Körner to meet him. Soon the pair converged towards a twilight wood, sparsely grown with bare oaks. The bald monk waited in this deserted place and soon he saw a rider approaching. When the newcomer was close enough he could be recognised as the Dark Knight, Maximilian Körner, clad in his black hussar rig with the death's head emblem on his fur hat, riding a dapple-grey horse. Körner reined in his horse where Morven was waiting by the roadside.

"Thank you for coming, Dark Knight."

"At your service, master," Körner said with a discreet salute.

"Right, I've failed too," said Morven, straight to the point. "Yes indeed, even I have failed in my attempt to ensnare this Grey Knight. And now he has The Rose That Never Fades. Nothing seems to have worked for us so far. We are doomed, unless –"

"Aha," Körner interrupted, "so it's up to me then to attack him? Maybe I'll try –"

"Stop. No more child's play, no more fancy creatures or clever ploys to trap him. What we need now is nothing less than to levy an army, an army of darkness, a rabble of hangmen and torturers, a throng of murderers and arsonists who will be talked about forever. It will be our final line of defence against this Griffensteen and his mission."

"To raise an army just to stop Griffensteen?"

"It will be of greater use," continued Morven. "With it we can also take control of The Land and all other astral lands in the cosmos, and then by their correspondence with the minds of men all everyday lands too, all human existence forever!"

"Clever," agreed Körner. "Yes, excellent. But how will this be done? How do we recruit such an army?"

Morven looked up at the grey sky, admiring some dark clouds drifting by, and seemed lost in thought for a moment.

"You're a warrior, right, sworn to the Dark?"

Körner nodded.

"You have lived out life after life as the Dark Knight. And thus you came to know many villains throughout world history, traitors and wrong-doers and obscure fellows – the betrayer Ganelon, Johan Hastesko and the men of the Anjala conspiracy, the defector Benedict Arnold, bandit gangs and Death's Head hussars, the Pappenheimer warlocks and other tormenters of peasants…"

Körner nodded in agreement. "I know them and I am one of them. Well, not a traitor, but a Dark Knight nonetheless. So now you want me to go back in history, back through the omniverse to those previous lives and recruit my former comrades-in-arms for an army?"

"An army with which to storm the heavens!" Morven said, smiling sardonically. He swept out his hand over the dead wood and beyond. "All this will be ours, the whole world's glory will be ours and subject to the powers of darkness under Yaldabaoth as emperor and with you and me as leaders. We two shall become rulers of the Earth! I shall be, let's see, the Proconsul and you'll be my field commander, the Crown Marshal. Nice title, eh?"

Körner stood silently waiting as Morven continued his tirade, working his way up to ecstasy.

"To rule with a rod of iron we must drum up an army with boots on the ground, an army of the Dark, and you're the one to do it. Me, I'm more of a chancellor, one who controls all the hidden plans and manipulations from the sidelines. However, you're the soldier, you move about in the outer world, you know its ways, you speak the language of both the ranker and the commander and you have all the contacts. Recall your past lives as a sombre soldier – you've done your fair share of dirty work. Besides the black hussar dolma you've carried the black cross too, the epitome of dark energy. You've been a knight of timeless orders, chasing and killing pagans as your prey. Pure slaughter. These among many other things, you have done, Maximilian Körner, my friend."

"And what else have I done?" Körner asked. He knew most of it but there had been so much, and no-one can remember every life they've led.

"Well, you executed Vercingetorix for a start. You're the trooper who killed Gustavus Adolphus with a stab in the back. You sacked Lübeck as a Napoleonic soldier during those three indescribable days. 'Cry havoc and let slip the dogs of war', that's you in a nutshell."

"I see."

"Now, the main thing is that you can go back in time and recruit the riff-raff and bandits, reconnect your acquaintance with the rabble of history and levy an army that will make us lords of the omniverse. And along the way we'll stop Griffensteen's progress."

"Where shall I gather the army, then?" Körner asked.

"It can garrison here, in this no-time and no-place. I'll have the logistics and operational plans arranged. But the hands-on recruitment of the army is your first priority now. So the sooner the better, off you go in The Land, this dimension of astral crossroads and junctions, and take a grand tour through the past to recruit forces to our cause. Along the way you can send lieutenants to do your bidding and recruit other fighters, such legendary villains as the black magicians Frater Perdurabo and Klingsor and all. Gather men and arms. And remember, Pelagion and Griffensteen are our enemies."

"But Pelagion was a neutral angel, wasn't he?" Körner mused, having been at Castle Munte himself, listening in on the angel's tale.

"Oh, that was just in order not to upset Griffensteen too much. Had they sent one of the good angels you would all literally have been blinded by the light."

"I guess Griffensteen was dazzled quite a lot anyway."

"What about you then?" Morven said. "Could you stand seeing the light of this so-called neutral angel?"

"Well, yes, it was a bit hard to endure, all that radiation. But I steeled myself against it, remembering the darkness I serve."

"I thought you would," Morven said smugly.

They said goodbye and rode off, Morven to his castle and Körner into history, in order to levy the army of the Dark.

Having parted ways with Morven, Ivan and Carl had set off to the Flowery Meadow to meet Pelagion as prearranged for when the Rose had been found. And as if by intuition or divine guidance, the field was eventually reached, a beautiful flowering meadow near a lake lined with aspen and linden. The water's surface was still. A sun stood high in the sky and a cuckoo cried in a copse some distance away.

"Such an idyll!" Ivan exclaimed.

Carl got off his horse and sat on the grass, shaded by some aspen, Ivan following his example. The colour of the sky was a rich, saturated teal. Among the leaves of grass there grew bluebells, buttercups and daisies. The trees' leaves were still, not even a rustle was heard nor the slightest gust of wind felt. Carl took the opportunity to meditate, finding peace within. As usual his mantra was 'I am'.

Having settled his mind, he then chanced to peer up into the sky, the lofty firmament, and into the faraway haze. Suddenly he saw some objects approaching. They flew high, they were small and he wondered what on Earth or Land they could be. As they came closer they lowered. Now Carl and Ivan saw that they were some kind of large silvery disc on which people were standing, five discs in all coming in to land and touching down simultaneously. The soldiers were stunned and speechless for a moment, looking at each other in bewilderment. Then Carl rose to his feet and started to approach the nearest disc, followed by Ivan.

There were people on the vessels. When they had landed one could see that the people were sumptuously dressed in kaftans of violet, blue and red with elaborate gold embroidery. On their heads they wore mitres, jewelled crowns and turbans. Carl bowed low and gestured to Ivan to do the same. "Welcome, strangers," he said, standing again. A figure in an orange mitre adorned with a ruby nodded his thanks. "Who are you?" Carl asked.

"We are the Essential Ones," the figure said. "We come from Ghislane, the glorious city where Pelagion is waiting for you. My name is Fasel. We've come to take you there."

"We are honoured."

"But... the horses?" asked Ivan, always the practical one.

"They can come along too."

The two men led their steeds aboard the silvery shimmering discs, Carl on the one travelling with Fasel and Ivan on another. When all the Ghislanians were ready, Fasel and the captains on the other four vessels bumped their rods on the decks. With this command the enigmatic craft silently took off, soaring into the rich, blue-green midday skies. They flew far over The Land and saw forests, fields, dark lakes and misty horizons.

"How far from Ghislane are we now?" Carl asked his host after a while. Fasel smiled indulgently.

"Nothing is so very far."

The vessels swished through the sky through light and shade, in the eternal no-time of The Land. The knight stood and looked fixedly ahead into the infinite spaces. Eventually, in the middle of nowhere, Fasel asked him if he could see anything. Carl tried to focus his gaze.

"Oh, yes, indeed!" he then said. "It looks like a blue spot in the ocean of space."

"It's the place we're going to," said Fasel. Then somewhat later Fasel asked the same thing. "Do you see anything?"

"Yes," said the Grey Knight. "I see a light in the blue spot and it shines like a star."

"It's the city we're going to," said the craft's commander. "Ghislane." And again somewhat later he asked, "Do you see anything?"

"Now I see a city that shines with crystalline splendour," Carl observed excitedly.

"So now we've arrived," said Fasel.

They approached the city, a city shimmering in the ethereal confluence of the omniverse, the legendary Ghislane. It had opalescent palaces with turrets and towers and translucent temples, silvery pavilions and lush parks, a jewelled floating city in an astral ocean. The five discs slid forward and landed on a square right in the city centre. Having stepped off the vehicles, the horses were taken care of and the men led along a street lined by tall houses with windows of crystal. People dressed in patterned silk greeted them guardedly wherever they went. Carl and Ivan answered their greetings.

"So this is the floating city that you and Yoritomo were told about?" Carl asked Ivan.

"It seems so."

"But you never found it yourselves?"

"No, it's not easy to find is it? And I guess we had to find the Rose first anyway."

"True."

Finally they stood before a huge white palace adorned with amber and jade.

"Where are you taking us?" Carl asked Fasel.

"To our rulers," was the simple reply.

Once inside the palace they were led up a broad marble staircase and passed through a stately room, the floor of which was so burnished that it looked like the surface of water. At long last they came to a large hall with porphyritic pillars. At the distant end of the hall, a figure on a throne could be discerned. They went up to him, bowed low and then faced him, the ruler of Ghislane; he was a tiny, wrinkled, wily gentleman in a blue kaftan with ruby applications. He sported long white hair with a headband and a closely cropped beard.

"Welcome, discoverer of The Rose That Never Fades," he said.

"Ah, how...?" stuttered Carl.

"I know one thing and another," the ruler said. "By the way, my name is Tacfarina."

"I am Carl Griffensteen, sometimes called the Grey Knight. This is my squire, Ivan."

"It's good to meet you both. And I apologise for having picked you up and flown you here, but I'm rather old and don't feel like moving around too much these days."

"The pleasure is all ours," said Carl. "It's beyond imagination to have seen this floating city, so rich in palaces and temples. I'm overwhelmed."

"I'm delighted to hear it. Soon we shall meet Pelagion, the reason for your journey here. But first, some food."

They were led to a chamber where they were given truly angelic food to eat, ambrosia and lotus bread. Afterwards, they were told that Pelagion awaited them in another chamber and having walked along seemingly endless shimmering corridors they reached a bronze chamber with a marble floor. There Pelagion awaited them, sitting on a couch, the deva as usual clad in a blue-green frock with a golden belt, on his head the frontlet with silver medallion. The angel congratulated them for having found the Rose.

"Don't you need to see it?" Carl asked, preparing to take it out of his tunic.

"I believe you," said Pelagion. "This kind of thing you can't lie about. And anyway, I can read minds."

"Aah."

"You will need this Rose on the next part of your quest. But what is that quest? This is a rather long story that needs to be told. Long and fascinating, if I may say so."

Carl and Ivan sat down on another couch nearby while the angel became quiet, preparing for his story-telling.

"I will now tell you a legend," he began, "the story of how all things began, and then onto other interesting developments and affairs concerning the state of the omniverse now."

The angel began telling the story of the moral history of the cosmos, a story of good and evil, of the Light and the Dark. The first part told about how God was in the beginning and how he created a son, Yaldabaoth by name. But Yaldabaoth became a rebellious fellow, ignoring his father and thinking that he, Yaldabaoth, was the master of the world.

In the ensuing rebellion, Yaldabaoth and his children came to occupy a realm called Sheol, the Lowest Heaven, situated above the astral world. Above Sheol were subtler heavenly realms ruled by God and a second generation of angels created as a counterpart, the devas. Yaldabaoth and his children were asuras.

In the Ghislanic chamber, Carl listened carefully to the story. And he reacted in shock when he heard that one of the asura pairs were called Morven and Parysatis.

"But I've met them," Carl said, interrupting Pelagion's narrative. "And you saw the lady, too, at Castle Munte. So they are, what, gods? Supreme angels?"

"Indeed," Pelagion said. "They are dark angels in human form, having incarnated as human. I'll get to that."

Carl was more than a little perplexed at hearing this but he didn't get a chance to air his feelings, for now Pelagion continued his tale of the war in Heaven, of Yaldabaoth's continued rebellion against God. After the plants, trees and animals had been created as astral models, Yaldabaoth felt like creating another figure on the angelic pattern: Man, in short, a being to serve asuras.

This came to be. God advised against it but Yaldabaoth didn't listen. The specific creation of mankind took place in Sheol, the dark realm of the asuras, in the main city in a place called the House of Demiourgos, a grand mansion of black sandstone with roofs adorned by gargoyles. There was mankind created. He was later transferred to the Garden of Eden where God adopted him and gave him a soul, a part of his eternal Light. Thus Man would instinctively, by his very nature, strive for the Light.

Men turned their back on the asuras, who had thus lost out to God. By this time, of course, the Earth had been created and Man spread across it. The beings of Light, the devas led by the Logos, were active in this; by incarnating as humans they helped men and taught them philosophy, art and husbandry. The asuras didn't like this, since Man had at first been created to serve them, so they also wanted to incarnate in human form as a means to lead Man back into the dark realms. Specifically, it was Morven who had the idea.

CHAPTER ELEVEN
LET'S INCARNATE!

Dark water surged against a rough, barren and inhospitable shore (Pelagion said, continuing his story). Mist lay over the waters. The chilly air froze the marrow. This was in the infamous Sheol, the lowest heaven. In central Sheol City there now wandered some sombre, cloaked characters along the main street, lined with high, vaulted buildings decorated with astral beryl and obsidian, malachite and carnelian. The figures eventually entered one of the houses, the council chamber, Symposion by name. It had walls of obsidian, marble benches and a floor of red granite. Eventually the company spread out, twelve of the figures heading for the semi-circular benches, the thirteenth heading for the lectern overlooking the auditorium. This figure was mildly melancholic, yet now glowing and impassioned, a well-proportioned being with wavy light hair. It was Yaldabaoth himself, father of the asuras. His distinctive traits charmed everyone.

He looked out over his children, nodded to the female and male asuras in turn, then struck the table with an adamantine stick.

"Thank you for coming. We have gathered here today to decide the future of our cause, for the final realisation of our asurean strategy. It is our good son Morven who has the plan so I give the floor to him."

Morven was one of the twelve seated on the benches. He was bald and burly, almost a little portly, yet clearly strong and sturdy. His face had a constant, enigmatic smile, incongruous in an anguished countenance. He stood up and bowed to Yaldabaoth and the others.

"My friends, I've been thinking. Look at our dear Sheol, once so glorious but now veiled in vapour and mist, in darkness and smoke. We live in ruins and we have lost touch with our creation, mankind. Man is currently being governed by devas who teach him bright thoughts, dedicated worship and mystery sciences acknowledging the inner Light. This is carried out by devas incarnating among men, deva souls uniting with human foetuses and being born as men, able to live among the people as people, teaching them eye to eye. Yes, we asuras can fly like ghosts over the cities of men and exert an indirect influence, whispering virtual advice and exercising telepathy. This has an effect, too. But not enough."

At his lectern Yaldabaoth was listening to what Morven had to say, while absentmindedly looking around the hall and drumming with his fingers in what is fittingly called 'the Devil's drumbeat'. Yaldabaoth noted every word in his mind. He got the gist of Morven's exposition but he said nothing yet, letting the other continue.

"Humans today live in Atlantis," said Morven, "that great island in the Atlantic Ocean, and there they have built cities, practising handicrafts and adorning themselves in glory. It's a beautiful spectacle. We did well to create men. Therefore, my brothers and sisters, I think we asuras should start to incarnate among them too. Then our lives wouldn't be so bleak, we would live in real palaces, we could have slaves – in short, our lives would be more full. Everything would be more fun, more interesting. And thus, living human lives, we would be able to affect humans even more in our asurean direction to pursue black magic, idolatry and devilry!"

The asuras liked the sound of this. Sitting in their Sheolian hall they nodded assent to Morven's words.

But then, however, something strange happened. A voice was heard, a strong, spiritual voice that penetrated everything and everyone in the hall. It was the voice of God. He had the habit of talking to his wayward asurean children now and then, and now it was certainly again time. Having heard what Morven had said, God now spoke.

"No, my children, do not do this. Do not incarnate in the form of people. Instead, I advise you to make amends and return to our Seventh Heaven. This incarnation venture will only bring misery, both to you and to Man. Going into the flesh will only take you deeper into the darkness you're already living in."

"What about devas, then?" said Morven, looking around and addressing the voice. "They're incarnating, living in the flesh as human beings."

"True," God said, "but devas are aware of the dangers of it all, of the temptations that a mortal life brings. Whereas you who want the Dark, you will be led on an entirely wrong path if you implement this plan of incarnating. So my advice, again, is for you to reconsider, to choose the Light and happiness instead of the dark material world."

Then Yaldabaoth, who liked Morven's idea, interposed.

"But we mean Man no harm, we just want to forget our existence here. We want to live among humans and not languish here like astral layabouts."

There was no response to this, God having now returned home to His Eighth Heaven. He was not one to haggle. His children had free will to choose the Light and this they could do anytime; but again they had turned it down. Yaldabaoth therefore continued.

"So God has left us to it and good riddance. As for Morven's plan, I think it's totally feasible whatever God thinks. Well then, fine. I say this: the Earth is beautiful, the sun and rain make everything grow and it's an amusing garden totally different from our misty Sheol. Humans in their temples and palaces live better than we do. Man is dressed in beautiful clothes and jewellery, he controls kingdoms and he controls nature, reigning over land and sea, over animals and plants. We lack all this, living a travesty of a life. Therefore, let's incarnate, let's take human form."

A great cheer erupted. Astaphaios rose and cried out, catching the spirit of the moment.

"Hooray for Yaldabaoth and Morven! Towards a life as men, to glorious earthly times! Let's forget ourselves, let's incarnate!"

All asurean minds were united in this cause. There was no hesitation, God's objections having already been forgotten. So it was decided to begin to incarnate in human form. To achieve this, Yaldabaoth would travel around the Earth and unite the spirits of his children to unborn foetuses, joining their astral bodies to the auras of human embryos. By doing so, the memories of the asuras would be removed. However, a small residue of anxiety and fear was always left with these incarnated asuras. It was their nature, their way of being.

Asuras incarnated on Earth, starting with Atlantis. There, asuras in human form eventually became tyrannical kings, demonic priests and wayward mystics. And all this sin finally resulted in the fall of Atlantis. But after the deluge, the literal sinking of Atlantis, some managed to escape to America, Europe and North Africa through Egypt; and thus the contest over mankind by devas and asuras, both now incarnated in human form, continued. Devas taught art and music, poetry and painting; asuras taught desire and violence, black magic and fear. This went on despite spiritual leaders being born, making something of a fresh start possible, although asuras with Yaldabaoth at their head continued doing what they could to stop the progress of Light. Incarnating as humans, they eventually became tyrants and wayward bishops and criminal operators of every kind.

But Yaldabaoth, for his part, couldn't incarnate because of being unable to forget himself, unable to erase his own asurean memory. So now he was lonelier than ever, wandering alone around the globe, all the time hating and cursing God, his father. God heard and saw it all.

"Stop this, my son," He said to him, seeing his first-born son sitting on a rock in a desolate mountain country. "I love you as you are. I forgive you. And here's an idea for what you can do about your life – approach Man and repent, try to win human forgiveness. To seek exculpation for the evil you've done is always possible. On the other hand, just cursing everything and everyone is leading you nowhere – on the contrary, it's leading you deeper into the Dark. That you curse Me, I forgive immediately, but that you're pulling darkness over yourself, that's where danger lies. Moreover, you're inveigling Man to do the same, to indulge in darkness when he should affirm the Light within. I don't understand what you're up to. Your life is monotony. Aren't you tired of hate and slander, death and loneliness?"

But Yaldabaoth wasn't listening. God couldn't force Yaldabaoth to be happy, to turn to the Light, it had to come from him. God had abstained from some of His power, some of His omnipotence, in order to allow both angels and people to follow their free will, a will that could be directed at both things material, by desire, and things spiritual. Yaldabaoth was the Prince of Darkness and proud of it despite the moments of frustration when he felt deserted by all and sundry, living alone.

> Which way I fly is Hell, myself am Hell;
> and in the lowest deep a lower deep
> still threatening to devour me opens wide,
> to which the Hell I suffer seems a Heav'n.
>
> While they adore me on the Throne of Hell,
> with diadem and sceptre high advanced,
> the lower still I fall, only supreme
> in misery; such joy ambition finds.

So farewell Hope, and with Hope farewell Fear;
farewell Remorse, all Good to me is lost;
evil be thou my good; by thee at least
divided empire with Heav'n's king I hold...

JOHN MILTON, *PARADISE LOST, FOURTH BOOK*

Yaldabaoth spread his wings and flew down to Earth. Once at the island kingdom of Atlantis, while it still thrived, he saw that his children had not been idle: they lived like princes and priests, spreading violence and heresy throughout the land. Yaldabaoth enjoyed this in the core of his asurean soul; he ventured about like a shadow, taking the opportunity to whisper devilry in the ears of the people.

So evil rose, the darkness spread and even good priests and philosophers were tempted and initiated to its weirdness. Little wonder then that this Atlantis soon went astray and literally broke up in earthquakes and deluges, finally being flooded and drowned by the sea, becoming prey to the waves. Some Atlanteans, both good and bad, escaped the devastation and made their way to the islands of the west, towards what would later become the Americas. Central America received many talented people and, the ground having been prepared by the previous Lemurian emigration, became rich with seers and pyramid builders, mystics and crystal technicians.

CHAPTER TWELVE

SEARCHING FOR
THE GOOD MAN

"But enough with brooding on Atlantis," said Pelagion, sitting in Ghislane and telling his story. "Let's return to devas and their activity among humans. Some light must shine in on our story, don't you think? There has been enough of darkness, of Yaldabaoth and all that, for a while."

"Maybe so," said Ivan, "but there's so much for us to digest. Asuras and devas, Lemuria and Atlantis, the incarnation of angels in human form and God knows what else."

"Well, let's take a break, then." The angel called for servants to bring drinks and soon the three of them had goblets of nectar before them. They drank and chatted generally for a while. Then Carl just had to comment on the angel's story.

"This certainly is different from the Bible and all I've been taught."

"What is so different?"

"Everything! Or, well, it's perhaps reminiscent of the Bible but…"

"The approach might be a bit new to many listeners," Pelagion said, "but the narrative is true. And now that I've told you most of the story, the rest isn't so hard to fathom. Then I'll get to your role in all this, the main reason for your quest."

Carl nodded and tried to think of something wise to say. Instead, Ivan simply asked Pelagion to continue.

"Thank you, my friends," said the angel. "So Atlantis perished but Man lived on in the East and the West, in the Old World and the New. And devas were still active, teaching humans good things such as astronomy, ontology, poetry, architecture and sculpture. Man's everyday life was embellished with things such as marble statues, columns and arches, the art of poetry and singing and the knowledge that he lived in a world among many worlds, a virtual omniverse, and that there was more than just the material life since Man had an eternal soul, a spark of the eternal Light."

This might all sound fine, the angel continued, but the truth was that the dark teachings continued to live on alongside this. Human cultures certainly soon thrived in China, India, the East and the Mediterranean, with names like Babylon, Persia, Greece, Rome, Qin and Maurya, but all wasn't well. The asuras were still about, being incarnated within humanity, and directly or indirectly they led people astray. Many people had a very hard time in their everyday lives, having difficulties in finding any meaning in their existence. Often, 'the man on the street' seemed to have no-one who cared about him.

As remedy for this, spiritual leaders such as Jesus were born, teaching mankind that God is within, that we all have a divine spark inside. He taught men to love one another as brothers. He created a spiritual upsurge, a lasting raising up of Man despite the cruci-fixion; perhaps even this was a triumph, an everlasting statement. Christianity and other faiths thrived and the devas continued to lead mankind to Light and clarity, teaching art and music, astronomy and other sciences. True, Yaldabaoth was still around and the asuras continued to incarnate and exercise their dark deeds, but on the whole the human race proceeded on a better path.

In Heaven, God and one of His devas, Hiranya, were planning a spiritual revival, a way of ending the rule of the Dark forever. It was time for Man to become initiated into a higher vibration. Associated with this development was the question of Yaldabaoth's redemption.

God, having retired to an emerald green heavenly garden, called His angel son and asked him to sit beside Him on a soft, purple sofa. For his part, Hiranya was a resplendent being exuding a mild golden light, indeed, for which his Sanskrit name was given. He was somewhat reminiscent of Pelagion; however, Hiranya had nothing of Pelagion's neutrality or melancholy about him but was the spiritual embodiment of pure will, truth and mild passion. He had long brown hair, a firm yet compassionate countenance and was dressed in a golden robe with a light blue surcoat.

"Son, I have an idea," began God. "It's this – wouldn't it be possible to save Yaldabaoth through a human intervention?"

"Maybe," Hiranya said. "Go on."

"I believe it can be done," God said. "It would suffice for the prayer of one man to save his soul. The loving thoughts of the prayer would attract Light to him, regret would be awakened in him and so, by his own will, he would be carried away from Sheol and brought home to the higher Heaven."

Hiranya contemplated this but was in two minds about it.

"How to find such a man willing to pray for Yaldabaoth? Everybody hates him, even though we devas may love him as the brother, sibling and cousin he is."

God, of course, had a plan for it all. First he sent Hiranya to walk the Earth to find this one, especially good man. He even took other devas to help him, and when this didn't result in anything he asked the neutral angels for assistance. One of them was Pelagion.

"However, neither could I find this one man able to pray for Yaldabaoth's salvation," the angel continued, sitting in the

Ghislanian palace, "until one day I eventually found a fine candidate in 1917, a man riding along a Transylvanian road up to Castle
Munte who could help with the quest…

"I saw you, Captain Griffensteen. You could find this admirable
fellow. The one who must find this good man, this intercessor, is
you."

"What? Who, me? Why?"

"Yes, you, Captain. By finding The Rose That Never Fades
you've proved your mettle, showing that you're both wise and
brave. So now for the next part of your mission, a task of an even
more spiritual kind – to find the one good man in the whole world
who can pray for Yaldabaoth, Lucifer, the Prince of Darkness.
Thus the whole world may be redeemed, evil will die out and Man
will live in peace, harmony and beauty forever."

So Pelagion had finished his story of the Light and the Dark,
of God, devas and asuras, of the creation of Man and more, and
had wrapped it up by saying that Carl Griffensteen's next mission
was to solve the world's crisis. Carl, listening with fascination to
the story in the Ghislane palace, where he had arrived by riding
through The Land seeking and then finding the Rose, now found
that this story was about himself. Or rather, that the next chapter
in it was to be written by him!

It seemed like a difficult task, to find such a good man. It was
a truly spiritual quest and he, Carl, was no saintly spirit. Then
again, he had his esoteric understanding and beliefs, and at least
he could try, he thought. He liked challenges and that's what had
brought him here to Ghislane in the first place. Without further
ado he made up his mind.

"I will find your man. I will try to find the good man."

"Fine, my son," the angel said. "And when you've found this
person, bring him to Sheol, seek out Yaldabaoth and start praying,
forgiving him and drawing the Light to him. We believe this will
work."

Carl was amazed by the nature of the mission, to save the chief asura and to heal the world just by finding a praying man? But it had to be worth trying.

"Now," said Pelagion, rising, "I'm away to other worlds and to deliberate on some matters. How shall we counter the last moves of the Dark? I mean, you've met Morven and Parysatis in The Land so they know of your quest. The forces of evil will almost certainly gather to stop you. Well, we'll cross that bridge when we come to it. So farewell for now. If you need me, I'll be at the bend of the Placid River. Come there any time and I will be there, invoked or not. *Vocatus atque non vocatus, Deus aderit.*"[2]

Carl didn't know this line but he nodded nevertheless. Just as he was about to open his mouth in response, the angel dissolved into a silvery mist. The soldier was astonished at the sight but then, having seen so many fantastic things by now, he quickly gathered his wits about him.

"Seems like we have another mission," he observed, turning to Ivan. "This is phase two of our adventure. So let's leave this city, fly away and hopefully be able to mount our steeds and ride out to seek this good man."

Carl and Ivan bade their hosts farewell in Ghislane, were given some provisions for the journey along with their horses, and were shipped away on a disc similar to the one on which they had arrived. Eventually they landed in a meadow of The Land, soon then riding through forests and across fair valleys, all devoid of men. This seemed like a bad omen since they needed to meet people.

They had to find this good man, the man who would pray for Yaldabaoth, an intercessor. To this end Carl and Ivan, by way of

---

[2] Carl Jung would later carve this inscription above the door of his house in Kusnacht, Switzerland. "Called or not called, God will be there."

The Land and into all of the human omniverse, eventually visited the largest cities, crossed the most heartrending wilderness, knocked on the most derelict doors and visited the most obscure eremite dwellings, but to no avail. No-one they spoke to was willing to pray for the Devil.

They truly searched everywhere. They used The Land as a crossroads for their passages in and out of history with all that meant, going to this time and that to find a pious and strong fellow who could intercede for Yaldabaoth and redeem him. The Land being what it was, a dimensional gateway, by using it as portal to everything and everywhere the pair visited all of the omniverse, riding through every possible everyday world, every dream land and fantasy land, every conceivable domain of myth and legend and reality, all in order to find that man. But he just wasn't to be found.

Every promising candidate was found to fail in one or other respect: they deemed themselves unworthy, or they lacked the will, the thought or the courage needed for this enterprise.

Then one day, riding through The Land from one infinity to another, they espied a house shaded by an oak tree. The sun was shining overhead but the house was in comfortable shade under its protective tree. Hens were cackling in the backyard. It was a restaurant of sorts. They rode up, dismounted, went in and sat down at a table. Ivan admired the interiors of visible girders in the roof, the long oak tables with benches and the bare walls of dark fretwork. But Carl for his part stared dejectedly at the worn table top.

There wasn't any menu to choose from. The fare was stew, bread and beer and this is what they got, after a while. Having finished the meal Carl was still brooding, now staring into his beer mug for a change.

"What's up?" Ivan asked his friend.

"Nothing," the Grey Knight said at first. "Well, it's just that I think I've had it. How will I complete my mission, to find this good man? We have indeed sought him here, there and everywhere."

"True, that," Ivan agreed, recalling their recent rides into the past, into myth and legend and every instance of reality. "You couldn't say we've been idle!" He smiled but his master didn't see the merry side of it.

"This is too much!" Carl said, finishing his beer.

"Unless…" Ivan continued hesitantly.

"Unless what?"

"Maybe, well, it's you."

"I'm what?"

"Maybe you, Captain, are that good man?"

"Me?" Carl stared back in disbelief.

"Yes, you. You're the one who must pray for Yaldabaoth. You must rise to the occasion, start to gather the strength for this spiritual mission. You have to become that man. Come on, you can do it. You're already a good man, at least, the best man I know. So you can become even better. You create your own world, don't you, just like us here in The Land creating our environment by expressing our thoughts? And you have a strong will, haven't you? Well then, use that will and create yourself into the good man we've been asked to find. Use your will, man!"

Carl looked up from his mug, a glint playing in his eye.

"So…?"

"Yes, indeed," Ivan said and smiled to himself. This down-to-earth man had found the answer to their spiritual task, stumbling upon it serendipitously after having searched in all the possible and impossible worlds. "You're the man, Captain. The Rose we already have, the one Pelagion said could be used as a passport to Hell or whatever."

Carl gazed out of a window, seeing the fields lying placidly in the sunshine. Alright, he thought, I have to become that man, that pure-hearted intercessor, by using my will, thought and compassion. Now, I'm just a normal man, yet I have a spiritual vision. So I'll just put my determination into it. I shall decide to do it. It's like going into battle, with determination. And I must find in myself the other qualities alongside that, like compassion and brotherly love. I'll have to see Yaldabaoth as my brother, one whom I care for and whom I want to turn to the Light.

The hens were cackling, the oak leaves rustled faintly in a gust of wind and from the back the ordinary kitchen clattering was heard.

"I'll do it, then," said Carl, turning to his manservant and drawing himself up. "So help me God. My brooding days are over and we are going places – to Hell and to redeem Yaldabaoth." He folded his hands and prayed, meditating silently, being joined in this by Ivan. He wasn't really the praying type but now he tried.

"God, you of the Light of which my inner light is a part," Carl spoke softly, "show me the way in this final quest. Give me Light so that I am not tempted by the Dark. I shall do my best to complete my mission, and I shall try not to become prey to negativity. Help me and my companion in doing Your work. Amen!"

"Amen!" Ivan seconded the prayer. With this they got up from the table, paid for their meal and left, the hens scurrying out of their way. They mounted their horses and rode off in the midday heat to Hell.

CHAPTER THIRTEEN

PARYSATIS

They rode through a wood of birch, aspen and beech trees, the sun being sieved through the foliage bathing everything in a golden green hue, reminding Carl of a similar moment on the road to Castle Munte in another world, in another time.

"So then, on to Sheol," cried Ivan, riding alongside, "to the dark domain of this Yaldabaoth fellow, or whatever he's called. Um, where do we find Hell?"

"Good question," Carl agreed. "Maybe we could ask Pelagion again. Just go to the bend of the Placid River. He said we could always find him there."

The wood opened up before them, giving way to a field with quaint copses. In the distance a castle could be seen, a fairy-tale castle with high turrets, cupolas and intricate wings and fronts. Its walls were made of bronze and the roofs glistened with gilded copper.

"Maybe we can ask the way there," Ivan suggested. They decided that Carl should do this alone while Ivan would lie down in a meadow to rest, spending his time doing nothing and everything in the no-time of The Land. So Ivan disappeared into the greenery while his master rode on to the castle.

Carl approached the legendary Hortalion, also known as the Bronze Castle. By chance (or was it?) he had found Parysatis' abode, the one she had invited him to visit when they had first met at Castle Munte. Not realising this, Carl just felt it right to approach the place. It shone in the afternoon sun with a yellow glow tinged with red, a lustre like aurichalcum, the famed metal mined in Atlantis and also known as gold bronze; it had a fiery sheen not of this world, played off against the surroundings of red sandstone. Carl was bewitched by the form of the castle, its domes and towers, its spires and loggias and flying pennants. He rode along a marble road lined with sphinxes and pruned yews, the enigmatic stone guardians placed between shrubs shaped into spheres, cubes and pyramids. Once at the metallic castle, he rode in unchallenged through an archway, crossed a courtyard, dismounted and left the horse in a stable where there was a manger with filled troughs.

Carl proceeded to what looked like the main building and made his way into a spectacular lobby adorned with silver and platinum, which was a nice change to all the red metal outside. Then he sauntered on alone through halls and along corridors and galleries until he came to a veritable golden chamber upstairs with green wallpaper and carpets, golden lintels, gold brocade on the chairs and sofas and golden tracery around the ceiling. He halted by an arched window and looked out over the gardens. Beyond the greenery he admired the wilderness of the mountainous countryside. As the sun went down, the landscape then faded into a russet purple.

Carl heard footsteps behind him. Turning, he saw a brown-eyed woman approach, wearing an indigo dress with a red blouse, her dark hair shaped into an elegant wave. He recognised her immediately but to match the ambiguous mood of the moment he said, "Haven't we met before?"

"We have," the woman said. "Welcome, Carl Griffensteen."

It was indeed the woman he had first met at the dinner in Alexandru's castle, the mysterious Parysatis. She was an asura yet a penitent one, a dark angel in human form, now living in The Land as part of her repentance. Many of her asurean siblings lived the same way but what was unique about Parysatis was that her companion, Morven, still served the Dark. And Parysatis was still in contact with him. But there was something else special about being the ruler of the castle Hortalion, for this also meant being guardian of the Temple of Memory nearby. In a strange way, Carl had found his way to Hortalion and to Parysatis because the care she felt for him, a sisterly love and admiration, would urge him towards this place in order to find out about his past and bring him clarity concerning his place in the cosmos.

They went through to the garden where Carl approached Parysatis closer and took her hand, looking into her alluring brown eyes. He was almost struck dumb at the sight of her, with feelings he couldn't express. But of course, he thought, meeting an asura in beautiful human form doesn't happen every day. Now he needed to ask her about her relationship with Morven. Parysatis explained that the two of them didn't see each other so much these times.

"So you've separated?"

"Not quite. But, you know… I want to leave darkness and despair behind and move back to the Light." Well, maybe she spoke the truth, Carl thought. He was wary of her, having learned so much from Pelagion, but for now he let it go, allowing intuition to guide him as it had at so many other times during this adventure.

Parysatis brought him to a pavilion, a white octagonal building shaded by a giant tree. Inside was a table already laid with golden goblets and a bronze flask. The woman poured wine for them and they sat down to taste it.

"It's good to see you again, Captain. Maybe we could dance and play, but there's no time for that now. I have things to tell you. Instead, you need to head back out into the garden and there find your way to a certain small lake. Then you will cross the lake to reach an island of cypresses, also known as Flanagan."

"What…?" said Carl. Another mystery already and a thousand thoughts swirled in his mind, but he had no time to think.

"You need to go to Flanagan and enter the temple there, the Temple of Memory. Once there, you must read from the Book of Life. What you find will surprise you, I promise. It's of great importance for your personal development, as it were."

Carl drank his wine. He had wanted to relax for a while but apparently duty called again. As for that duty, Parysatis had said nothing about the Rose. Did she know, and was this another trap from the Dark? He couldn't know, yet the woman seemed sincere so he would do as she instructed and then, hopefully, return. He felt intuitively that it was important to go to this island and read the book.

"I shall do as you say," he said. Carl stood up, bowed and went out of the pavilion, venturing through the garden until he found the small lake Parysatis had told him about. In the water grew lilies. And in the middle was an island surrounded by cypress trees and with a white temple on the crest of a low hill. There was a low, wooden footbridge across the lake so without further ado Carl set off across the bridge towards the enigmatic Flanagan, the island of cypresses. The water was dark and quiet around him, golden brown clouds hung in the skies. Having arrived at the island the cypresses towered above him, enclosing him in their dark beauty. This was truly an island of death, he thought.

The 'Isle of the Dead'? Parysatis hadn't called it by that name. But it certainly had some deadly connotations, reminding Carl of Böcklin's recent painting. Now he was in it, or so it seemed. A hand of ice seemed to grasp his heart, a new experience for him. 'What is this? Am I afraid?' he thought. 'I, the Grey Knight, who fears neither devils nor trolls? In this place there's no magic, there's only darkness in the cypress trees and a white temple in front of me. Oh well, and perhaps death. So let's go and meet death…'

He walked up the path to the white temple, a simple square building of tasteful proportions. Once at the top of the steps, he turned around and looked out over the lake and the climes beyond. Somehow he seemed able to see everything, the whole of Earth's kingdom with all her glory, interlaced with an omniverse presence. He saw great forests and broad fields, endless seas and, scattered around it all, villages and towns. And it was as though he could see into every house, into every room; everywhere he saw people, the ordinary people sitting at their handicrafts and their meals. There were also people who didn't seem to be doing anything, their faces distracted and shining with an inner light, an unmistakable smile at the lips, a twinkle in the eye...

What was this, Carl thought, to be warmed by such a banal sight? There must be something wrong. However, to be warmed by the sight of the land of Man is not so trivial, seeing man's inner Light externalised. Having admitted the Light within himself, he was resolved that soon he would indeed pray for Yaldabaoth, once he had reached Sheol. Here he stood, enlightened, halted before the Temple of Memory and looking out over the world. Praise the Lord, to be of the same Light.

He turned back towards the entrance and went inside. In the bare, unadorned vestibule he took off his gun holster, sword belt and cap and then went through a simple doorway, ending up in a similarly plain hall. The marble had a warm tone and the proportions of the room were harmonious. At a low lectern beside a chair was placed a book, on either side a burning candelabrum. He walked up and sat, breathed out and read on the cover: The Book of Life.

'The Book of Life?' he thought. 'This can certainly make you feel humble. A book of life in a House of Memory, whatever that could mean.' He opened the book and found himself reading 'Chapter 7322: Silverstar'.

Carl read about a flame of life that was created in primaeval times, a 'soul spark' named Silverstar. That's me, Carl realised, my astral and eternal self, my soul name. At the same time as Silverstar, a twin beam came into existence, called Greensleeves. Silverstar and Greensleeves loved one another and lived together in bliss forever as a dyad, as a male and female twin essence. Like angels, humans were created in pairs according to the pattern of male and female. Carl intuitively understood now that all beings, from human and onwards, were created in pairs like this.

He read on about how something had come to draw Silverstar down towards dimmer, more tangible and material climes, his soul being wilfully attached to a human foetus, and that eventually he lived a life on Earth as a man. There were hard times with stone axes, wolf blood, hounds and screams, but also security in the cave where the firelight flickered across the walls. And then at last a fair creature had appeared in this life, a woman who soon became his wife. It was Greensleeves, who had also incarnated on Earth as a human being.

Carl sat in the temple and read about his previous lives, the continuous incarnations of the spirit Silverstar on Earth as a man. In his first ever earthly life he had been a caveman and a hunter, a venerated leader of his tribe, a grey-eyed Stone Age chieftain. Once, his twin soul, the fair Greensleeves, had fallen into his arms as a spoil of war.

Thus it continued in repeated cycles. After an earthly existence there came the return to heavenly meadows and sometimes a reunion there with Greensleeves, his soulmate. Sometimes they met on Earth, sometimes not; sometimes the one was left in Heaven while the other lived on Earth. Sometimes they met as lovers, sometimes siblings, sometimes just as friends; but they always had something to offer one another, contributing to the other's spiritual development. No meeting is the first and no farewell is the last.

Silverstar for his part lived many lives as a warrior. He was a column head in Pharaoh's army, he fought too in the front line behind a bronze shield on the Marathon plain, wearing a helmet and greaves and a loincloth, and in his next life he rode over the Persian plateau in search of Bessos; he also led his squadron against Indian elephants at the Hydaspes and finally, in this self-same life, he was at Alexander's bedside with bared head, at the Râja-ti-Râja death camp in a Babylonian palace while wheat fields beyond the city wall faded away in the faraways.

He was reborn, this soul called Silverstar, and was later to live a life as Carl Griffensteen; he was reborn to life after life and each life was a realisation of a predilection for war, horses, weapons, orders and marches, hardships and triumphs and defeats. His coat colour was grey, he liked this neutral colour, so it was successively repeated in items such as a grey headband, a grey shield, a grey tunic and a grey loincloth; it was the same trait that had him to become the Grey Knight in an adventure in The Land.

CHAPTER FOURTEEN

SILVERSTAR AND GREENSLEEVES

Carl read about his past lives and saw them being played out before him like a movie or an unusually vivid dream, for example a life as a crusader in Syria among a whole range of other lives. He saw himself in his previous incarnations living the soldier's life again and again and again; and he saw himself meeting a green-eyed woman, again and again and again. He met her as lover, husband, cousin and brother, as unknown admirer and in diverse other roles.

Once she was a nun and he was the head of a Grand Compagnie; as a mercenary he would escort her from one monastery to another in France, in the late 1300s. While riding through the countryside, they had a deep conversation about life and death, about the Light and the Dark. It was as if they had always known one another, as indeed they had. They were spiritual siblings, twin souls, this glorified pair of Silverstar and Greensleeves, forever together in spirit, sometimes together in earthly form. This day, when birds chirped, a brook glittered and the sun's rays filtered through the foliage of the oaks, they rode up to the Bourgogne monastery in the year 1382.

"But where do we go when we die?" asked Silverstar, in this life called Guillaume.

"You will go to Heaven," said Greensleeves, named Laureline. The horses' hooves stomped on the road's soil, the surface being rather hard after a prolonged drought.

"So maybe we…?"

"Yes, certainly," said Laureline, steering her horse past a fallen tree trunk. Guillaume looked at her hand and saw that she was wearing a ring with an engraved bird in jade. "We can continue this conversation in Heaven. We might even have done that before, like when we were created."

"How amazing."

"More remarkable things than that have happened."

They didn't, of course, remember their meetings in Heaven, except indirectly, and the conversation continued as they rode to the monastery, feeling kinship. Having arrived at their destination they parted, never to meet again in person. But they started to exchange letters about spiritual matters, with Laureline's guidance, for example, teaching Guillaume that the warrior's path wasn't necessarily a good one (though, of course, it was better to be a warrior for good than for bad). Their friendship remained, in this life, on the spiritual plane. Guillaume was eventually knighted for his services to France and he received a fief in Provence, married the daughter of a count and had several children. He felt some kind of love for his wife, no doubt, though in his heart he was constantly with Laureline.

She for her part never left the monastery. Shortly before she died, she sent Guillaume her jade ring, the one with the bird. It had been a family gift from the time before she entered the order of nuns. Guillaume received the ring gladly and, after matching it for his larger ring finger, he wore it all the time. His wife, with a tinge of jealousy, took it off him on his deathbed and put it away in a box, whence it was forgotten. But only temporarily. This ring would turn up again later.

In the early 19th century, Silverstar was living in America, a life in which Greensleeves was his cousin. They lived on neighbouring farms in Vermont and talked about light and harmony until Silverstar enlisted as a private in the regular army, donning the grey cloth uniform. As the war of 1812 broke out, he was sent to fight against the British at New Orleans, in the process being promoted to corporal and leading his men in an assault against a wall of lead. He fell and was lying in the shade of a sycamore tree as his precious blood enriched the fertile soil, drawing his parting groan while admiring the light filtered through the tree.

In his next life, as a Swede of the mid-1800s, Silverstar again showed an inclination towards a military profession but Greensleeves, as his older sister, advised him not to focus so much on riding and shooting but to study Mathematics and the Sciences. Thus he eventually passed all the Karlberg War Academy courses gallantly and could choose to serve in the Engineer Corps, the elite of those days. He ended up at the Svea Engineer Regiment in Gustavsberg, rose through the ranks to colonel and crowned his career as adjutant to King Charles XV. At this time the Swedish army wore dark blue uniforms. But in this career Silverstar was also involved in the early stages of the planning for the future m/1910 uniform which would be grey; so this was a foretaste of the Russian army tunic he would wear in his next life, the garb that ultimately would give him his omniversal nickname, the Grey Knight.

A grave is closed, a human life is ended, a soul is going to Heaven and a song resonates throughout the spheres. They would meet, he and she, once again in the Elysian Fields. "So how have you been…?" "Well, my dear soulmate…" and "Maybe we shall meet again down in that vale of tears…" "But why do you have to go…?" "Well I must fight a war, now and forever…"

Then it is time to choose a new life, and the next choice is made to live in the neighbouring country, eventually leading to a life in field grey in Saint Petersburg and Tysjatsaja Stakan, in Galicia and Moldavia, in Wallachia and Transylvania. And here Carl's chapter in the Book of Life ended.

The text Carl was reading had come to an end. The story of his life was, for the moment, paused; what remained of it wasn't written yet. Carl closed the book and rested his chin on his hands, thinking: indeed, this was an eye-opener. 'Do I always make war?' Apparently. In life after life. 'Will I never learn my lesson? Will I ever become a more free and gentle type, sing hymns and spread the Light to all? Well, I will try to do that now, by interceding for Yaldabaoth.'

He folded his hands and looked into the candelabra, seeing the light of life, the soul spark, the *scintilla animae*. To find peace… peace… peace. Just learn how to enjoy the moment. Breathe calmly. Feel the tranquility of living, come to rest. Relax. Find the peace of just being. Stop craving another warrior's life, and another and another.

The thoughts grew within him until he felt that he was dreaming, dreaming about feeling at peace about nothing, experiencing the joy of mere existence. He said to himself, 'Yes, I can think of other lives than to kill and be killed, ending up lying prostrate on a distant field and become food for crows. Another life than just receiving and giving orders, just enduring hardships, battle, toil and sweat.

'Well, I've been a good soldier, as far as I know. But I can also try to be more human, try to be a good man… and that's my current ambition.'

So then, onwards to the last leg of the mission, to find Sheol and intercede for Yaldabaoth.

He moistened his index finger and thumb and put out the candles by squeezing the flames, smothering the wicks between his fingertips. Then he rose and went out. The Land spread out endlessly before him, the sun shining down through a cloud and illuminating it all in white gold, shining over good and bad alike. Carl walked down the cypress hill, approached the footbridge and breathed freely, inhaling the aromatic scent of the trees and the water lilies. The water reflected the blue of the sky, deepening it to blue-green and tourmaline. As he returned to the Hortalion garden, the still lingering image of Greensleeves made him melancholy. Where was she now in this life? Lost in ethereal thoughts, he didn't remember that he had already met such a green-eyed woman in this life, both in The Land during this mission and in the earthly kingdom.

He suddenly found himself strolling through the Bronze Castle's gardens, his route passing the fountains, gazebos, flower borders and ponds. Soon the palace itself became visible beyond some exotic trees. He approached it, walked through an archway and arrived in an inner garden where Parysatis sat playing the flute. She stopped playing and looked up at him.

"Please sit down."

Carl did so.

"When the lord of this world blows it becomes winter, but when the Holy Spirit blows, it becomes spring," she said.

"So who is the lord of this world," Carl asked, "the one blowing the winds of winter?"

"It is Yaldabaoth, my former master."

"Former?"

"Yes. I once belonged to the powers of darkness. As you know, I was an asura, one of Sheol's inhabitants, one of those who led the human race astray. But realisation of the Light has led me to the other side. Aeons of meditation here in my palace have made me realise things and led me to intuitively follow the Light instead of darkness.

"And so you've switched sides, just like that?"

"The good comes unconditionally to this world. Spontaneously, good things evolve from the inner light. I've realised my own inner light," she agreed.

At first Carl, with his military mind, thought this sounded suspicious. But what would he do? He realised that he liked this woman who thrived in Hortalion, this Bronze Castle. He saw life, light and truth in Parysatis' eyes, not malice. And she had been right about the Palace of Memory, it had been right for him to go there. It hadn't been a trap.

"So what are you now, an incarnated angel?"

"Yes," said Parysatis, "in the form you know me, I'm human."

"What a thing to believe."

"Come, take a walk with me," she said.

They walked throughout the gardens with their forking paths, their pines and cypresses, plane trees and bushes, their chrysanthemums and anemones, ferns and mosses, their streams and fountains. Shadows and echoes enveloped everything in their magic; unheard melodies played in the bushes, unseen visions lingered in the gardens' vistas as they strolled along meandering walkways and wandered silently along branching trails. Eventually they came into the palace again, the legendary Bronze Castle, where they had an exquisite meal and then played before making love. In the morning Carl, woke up in a room of gold and blue silk. He saw Parysatis sitting at a table set for two. Carl got up from the bed, approached the table and looked over the misty park.

"I'm speechless."

"What about?"

"About what I read yesterday of my former lives." He turned back to Parysatis, appreciating her lovely countenance, and sat beside her.

"It's all right," said the woman, putting her hand on his. "You needed to know that."

"Needed to? Well, maybe."

They breakfasted on wine, plums and pastries, eating in silence. Carl for his part contemplated everything he had read in the Book of Life. He kissed his lady on her hand, smiled and thought that maybe he would stay here in her company. Chirping birds were heard. The wind was playing in a curtain. It was broad daylight outside.

Then Carl suddenly remembered that he still had his assignment; and that must come first, even if this might be an ever-so-sweet haven here, a fine paradise, a Garden of Eden with astral harmonics, right in the middle of The Land. He devoured the last pastry, drank from his goblet and again felt ready to ride out into The Land, this time literally to go to Hell! It was his task, finding and interceding for Yaldabaoth in the domain of Sheol. But how to get there?

"I wish I could stay but it's time for me to go. Still, one thing I wonder."

"What is it?"

"Where do I find Hell?"

"Ah, the dear Sheol…" said Parysatis wistfully. "The abode I once knew as my home, as the asura I was. Well, you see, Hell is not underground as most people think but above it."

"That rings a bell somewhere," said Carl, "It sounds like something I've heard before." He then told her what Pelagion had said to him in Ghislane, about Sheol being an astral abode above the Earth, the former lowest of the eight Heavens. And after Yaldabaoth's dark invasion of mankind on Earth this lowest Heaven became a shadowy and gloomy place, in short, Hell. And between there and the Earth was situated The Land, the astral world.

"Indeed," said the woman, "that's how it is. And the road to Sheol is surprisingly straightforward. There's a large tree beyond a rocky plain, Gnipaheden, known as the Evil Tree because it reportedly springs from the root of all evil. It's a tall tree, reaching up above the clouds, and inside the tree is a staircase; along the staircase you may reach Sheol."

"Is that really all there is to it?"

Parysatis simply nodded. Carl was preparing to get up and leave. The woman naturally became curious and asked him what business he had in Hell.

"Oh, I'm going there to save mankind," answered Carl enigmatically, "and increase the Light in the world. Just like you seem to be doing."

"True," said Parysatis. "I live in the Light now, increasing it with my will, by my thought and passion. I live to discover, to marvel, to sing and dance – you know, like now, looking out over the beautiful misty climes of dawn. Perhaps even this is my adventure, whether or not I have an important mission right now, like you. It's an endless adventure, an everlasting adventure. That's what living means, to live all our lives, to love the place and love the moment, whenever that moment or wherever that place may be."

Having taken leave of Parysatis, Carl went outside, mounted his steed and rode away from the mysterious Hortalion. He approached the meadow and the copse where Ivan had waited for him, the fellow now sitting on a moss-covered stone sunbathing.

"It's time," Carl said. "Are you ready?"

"At your service," Ivan said, going to fetch his horse which was grazing nearby. "Where to?"

"To Hell, by way of Gnipaheden."

They rode off through the psychological lands, the terrains and milieus shaping themselves after their mood in the characteristic fashion of The Land. Thus, they first rode through a hardwood forest, then a forest of pine and spruce and next over a sandy moor grown with heather and moss. The terrain shifted in brownish violet as a cold wind blew and in the sky a bird circled. Ivan halted.

"Is that an eagle?" he said, gazing upwards.

"Hmm," Carl said when he, too, had halted his steed, "I'd say it's a buzzard. A subarctic vulture, a devourer of carrion."

They crossed a heath, a heartrending land with only sparse pine and yew. Indeed, there were some anemones and cloudberry flowers but other than that the heather dominated, a plant keeping its tiny petals even in winter, a plant characteristic of these desolate places.

"So is this Gnipaheden?" Ivan asked while they rode.

"No," Carl said, "as far as I can tell, it's not. These are just the approaches to it."

At nightfall they camped by a wooded hill, being protected from curious eyes by a giant five-metre high rock and surrounding shrubbery. This was sorely needed since the night lands gradually seemed to be teeming with horses and men, complete columns of battle-ready units sporting torches and banners. The next day, the two men therefore made a detour through the woods, wondering about the war cohort they had seen and discussing it. At last they rode up a hill where they halted, protected from view by the coniferous trees growing on top of the ridge.

They could see for miles. And in the distance they saw a subarctic plateau, surrounded by steep cliffs and even more harsh and devoid of greenery than the place where they themselves stood.

"Gnipaheden, I guess," Ivan said.

Over The Land, columns of men and riders were seen. These were their enemies, the armies gathered by Körner, now levied and ready to be deployed, intent on stopping them from getting to Sheol. The gateway to Sheol lay beyond this area. Carl and Ivan didn't expressly know that the gathering army was there to stop them, but they soon began to surmise it by the heavy darkness that hung in the atmosphere all about.

Leaving the outlook post, they kept going on towards the fateful plain, following a brook and protected from view by the hill. All the time they could hear the noises from the gathering armies. And, in the sky, black clouds gathered. Soon there was thunder and rain so the pair dismounted and waited it out under the friendly, dense branches of a spruce. There was lightning in the sky, there were rumbles across The Land. Carl gathered his wits and speculated about the enemy they had before them, but he was confident that he could defeat it somehow. They were in grim lands and a strange force was gathering but he wouldn't let this lower his spirits, not after having been through The Land, the past and every possible world in search for the Rose and then 'the good man', finally realising that he was that man. And the Rose he still held, keeping it in the inner pocket of his tunic, needed as a ticket for the journey to Hell.

So this man wouldn't allow some riff-raff army to stop him. But of course, he couldn't defeat it single-handedly.

CHAPTER FIFTEEN

ROADBLOCK ON THE ROAD TO HELL

The thunder and rain subsided, making way for clear skies and aromatic smells in the surroundings. The pair rode on under hazy skies, going up a rocky hill slope and finally reaching stony land close to the plateau. Leaving their horses in a cleft they quietly made their way closer, protected from view by rocks, all the time hearing the shouts of men and the noises from the horses and wagons. Having reached the flat land they crouched down on a mossy spot behind some boulders. In the sandy, stony field they saw an army deployed, thousands of men, dense formations of infantry and cavalry. Carl soon got the picture.

"It's a hellish host, having learned about our mission by way of Morven, probably, or whoever. What matters is that here they are, and this army is stopping me from going over Gnipaheden and getting to the gateway to Sheol."

Indeed it was Morven who was behind this hellish army gathering on the plain, part of his plans to rule The Land. He had given Maximilian Körner the orders to gather an army of the Dark after he, Morven, had failed to stop Carl at the River of Fire. The orders given to Körner when the two of them met in the twilight oak forest were to recruit the most evil army of history. The German had obeyed and started out on this mission, gathering a large unit of perjurers, butchers and perpetrators of madness. He had collected many odd characters under his grotesque Rat Banner. Now he had in his service, among many others, the gadget maker Bestos Fokalion; he had Ganelon who had betrayed Charlemagne; he had Cronstedt who betrayed Sveaborg; he had Benedict Arnold who had planned to betray West Point; he had murderers and arsonists and thieves and loose people recruited for blood money; he had the Sinner, Vasto the Vampire, Klingsor and Mordred, he who had killed King Arthur. Körner had levied forces from The Land, from legend and from history, and by virtue of spreading rumours even more hellish hordes had eventually gathered, promising to make this the greatest battle ever fought.

The scum of the omniverse had come together to prevent Carl in his task to redeem Lucifer. If he succeeded with it, these fiends would lose their lord and master and would become spiritual orphans. Then they would be unable to continue their devilry, neither in this world nor in our world and nor in every other, parallel world of the omniverse confluence.

Carl and Ivan looked at the army of the Dark, deployed in strength before them. They saw black armour and horn helmets, Thames scramasaxes and daggers, they saw snares and whips, packs of dogs and flocks of magpies hovering above it all. They saw laughing demonic faces, distorted human features, evilly grinning ghouls and fearsome floating vampires; and they saw banners adorned with skulls, crows and bats in a veritable heraldic hell, above them all the Rat Banner flying as the army's rallying flag, displaying a big, black rat on yellow background.

"What can we do?" asked Ivan. "Beyond Gnipaheden is supposed to be the tree you told me about, that tree we have to get through so we can reach Sheol."

Carl thought calmly for a moment.

"True. The road to Sheol is blocked by this army. We'll have to go and seek Pelagion. We must ask our dear deva for advice." These words were weighed carefully; this was the only option open to them.

"But, um, how?"

"When we met in Ghislane, he told us we could seek out the bend of the Placid River if we needed to talk about something, if we needed another piece of advice."

"Oh, yes," agreed Ivan, "you're right. So be it. Well, off we go then?"

"We do."

They sought out their horses, led them down the slope, mounted and rode away from Gnipaheden. Having to seek out Pelagion one more time, they rode for the bend of the Placid River with no clear idea of where it might be. But as usual, riding through The Land's mental landscape, through the no-space of its psychological clime, it wasn't long before they reached the site they sought. In a pastoral neighbourhood near a river, the deva was found sitting on a granite throne on a small hill, a round and elevated grassy knoll from which one had a view of the river as it lazily floated along in a curve against a backdrop of spruce and birch. In the distance, blue mountains could be seen.

Ivan and Carl dismounted in the meadow and let the horses go down to the water to drink. They themselves waved to Pelagion, the deva smiling back in a melancholy fashion at the circumstances of this last reunion; for it would now irrevocably be their last meeting, the soldiers needing some final good advice about how they would reach Sheol. They knew the way all right, but the road was blocked by the army of the Dark. If no other advice could be received, Carl thought, only one thing remained to do: to stand or fall, by riding straight into the bandit army, with the Rose as his banner, and believing in the truth of his cause.

They went up the hill and bowed to the deva. Pelagion was his neutral self, cool and firm in his blue-green robe and silver frontlet. He gestured for them to sit down on two wooden chairs already placed next to the stone throne. The pleasantries having been exchanged, Carl presented their dilemma: how could they break through the demon army that barred the way?

"It's simple," the deva said quietly. "You must raise your own army. And that will be done by you, Carl, going back in time and talking with old squires and comrades-in-arms. I know you've just seen your previous lives and I know everything, or almost everything, about you. I also know that you've realised that you are the good man we need, the one to intercede for Yaldabaoth."

At these words, Carl relaxed a little. He seemed to be in good hands with this deva as chief advisor, one who clearly saw all that was happening from above. But before Carl could say anything, Pelagion continued.

"And you, my dear Ivan, you should head to all the places in The Land where you have been, where you've ridden back and forth in search of the Rose, for your path is marked by good men, by true sword arms that would love to make an effort for the Light. The Land is a nexus of all realities and non-realities, a crossroads of myths, legends and sagas. Go visit all these realms, Ivan, and recruit willing swordsmen, adventurers and heroes. They are there, they are waiting for this. And, by spreading the word, more and more recruits will come along, led by the need for strength. The same goes for the levying in history. You Carl, by presenting the task, eventually will reach others by word of mouth and rumour and hearsay."

The angel paused, allowing them to take in the enormity of their tasks.

"Tell it like it is, both of you," he went on. "Tell the truth when you're trying to recruit people. Say that you fight for truth and justice, for the Light and for life against darkness and chaos. This is a battle that could determine the history of the world, indeed the whole of the Earth's, The Land's and all of cosmic existence. With a victory of the Light, Earth will live on and prosper in greenery and wellbeing. But with a victory of darkness we're facing decline and decadence, sterility and death.

"But this isn't all," the angel continued. "You must win at Gnipaheden and then continue beyond, to complete your mission to redeem Yaldabaoth. You must find your way to Sheol, either after the battle is done or by breaking through the barrier of the bandit army. I'll leave that to you. However, once through you're on your own and must remember this too – it's not about staging a veritable invasion of Hell, this is not the way, not by force of arms should Yaldabaoth be convinced but with the spiritual power of compassion. It's about the good man going there, finding Yaldabaoth and praying for him."

"I hear and acknowledge," Carl said, bowing his head. "We will do as you say. As for the levying plan, it's a good way, yes, a brilliant way, to enlist old squires in time and space. In and out of history and fairy-tale, from all over the omniverse. This will truly be the greatest battle in history, myth and legend, all in one and one in all."

Pelagion nodded, adding, "Who will lead the army of the Light?"

"Me, I suppose," Carl answered.

"Do you think that's wise?"

"But shouldn't I myself lead the army I've levied?" Carl said, surprised.

"Well," said the angel, "your primary task is to ride on further. And someone has to lead the army while you're intent on doing that."

"I see," said Carl. "You're right. I'll recruit an army, including an officer to act as my commander."

"Fine," said the angel. "The battle is one thing, your journey to Hell another. These two are linked but to have a dedicated army commander will ease your burden."

Carl and Ivan both nodded and bowed where they sat. Pelagion wished them good fortune in their missions, in their rides beyond the beyond, Ivan into myth and Carl into history. Intuition would lead them and the belief of the righteousness of their mission would be their guiding light. They had faith, they had the will to succeed. The deva made a final gesture of blessing over them and then was gone, spirited away to the higher Heavens.

And now the time for talking was over, indeed, the end of all discussion and planning, of all advisors and holy eminences. It was all now in the hands of Carl and Ivan, going silently down the hill, stepping up into their saddles and without further ado riding off in different directions.

Carl for his part rode in a trance through a sparse pine forest, hearing echoes from the past and watching the passage of clouds in the sky. He rode out in the wake of his previous lives, this grey rider on his black horse, the Grey Knight. That was his name, this was the legend he was becoming, indeed, that perhaps he had always been, as his chapter in the Book of Life had told. He was grey as the uniform that he, in one way or another, had always worn, and now he ventured back in time, following the echo of his omniverse existence.

He passed through a mist and came to a different country, a neighbourhood with terebinth and cedar trees in the Mesopotamia of the past. He had ended up in history, in a place where he had lived before. More to the point, he came to a military camp in the walled city of Babylon; he rode in and soon was talking with his old comrades of Alexander the Great's army, gathering them in a courtyard where he delivered his speech about the battle between the Dark and the Light that was to be fought on Gnipaheden. Clad in grey tunic, grey-blue breeches with red stripes, boots and service cap, Carl, a champion of light against darkness, simply asked them to follow him as their spiritual leader in the coming battle, with Earth's fate in their hands. He managed to recruit many of his former comrades and they duly followed him, sturdy ancient infantrymen in linen armour, bronze helmets and sandals and armed with swords and spears. At the same time, the word about the upcoming battle was spread to other camps in history and time.

Carl gave the pezhetairoi foot soldiers directions to an assembly area west of Gnipaheden, a place where five roads met. Then Carl continued his ride through history, proceeding through shady alleys and echoing vaults, ending up in Syria near the mediaeval castle of Krak des Chevaliers, the crusader keep basking in golden rays of sunset. He rode up the winding road, presented himself and his errand to the guards and came to the courtyard where several knights happened to sit in the saddle, preparing to go out for a reconnaissance mission. The man in charge of the troupe was Eustace le Jeune, a man Carl had served with in this castle as an 11th century crusader. Eustace wore a sword belt and a conical helmet without a visor, showing his bearded visage and innocent yet firm look as a pious warrior and a leader of men. Over his chainmail he wore blue livery dotted with golden fleurs-de-lis. He recognised his old friend immediately and greeted him.

"Brother! I need your help," said Carl. "There's a battle looming, a battle against darkness and death. Will you come with me and fight for light and life?"

"Indeed?" le Jeune said, curious.

"A battle between good and evil is in the offing and I need your help," Carl continued. "I have The Rose That Never Fades as my token and I am bound for Hell itself, to redeem the Devil. But the way is blocked by a diabolical force, a satanical army of torturers, bandits and rat catchers. I need good fighting men! We must defeat Hell's army, we must break the powers of darkness. If they win, they will pull the Earth down into darkness and confusion, chaos and despair, decay and death. But I fight for the Light and for life. So I ask you all to come and fight for your life and for a good future for Earth and for all of humanity!"

The crusader accepted the request on the spot and commanded his men to follow the Grey Knight. They rode off and passed again through the climes of The Land, this crossroads of cultures, where Carl directed them to the assembly area west of Gnipaheden, telling them that he would soon be with them.

Next he rode through a hardwood forest that brought him to a brick-walled courtyard at the Bohemian castle where Carl had been placed as an imperial cavalryman during the Thirty Years' War. Here he met old squires with heavy muskets, he saw cavorting horses and six-pound shells, and he gathered the men before him and recruited them for his cause.

Carl wasn't finished yet. He rode through a pine forest, eventually finding a camp of soldiers in blue and yellow and with triangular felt hats; and he rode through sycamore woods and found warriors in grey and dark blue; and he rode into a stone city and found soldiers in modern tunics with brass buttons and waxed moustaches. And everywhere he levied troops, constantly increasing his entourage, and they all followed him through the dimensions and eras to end up west of Gnipaheden, joining the army of the Light. And by rumour even more soldiers gathered, the news being spread through time and no-time like rings on the surface of water.

He rode throughout history, following the tracks of his old incarnations, and at each site he gathered some listeners and spoke to them; he told the old comrades in time and space what he had said to the crusaders, the legionnaires and others. And they followed this Grey Knight, the legionnaires, knights, horsemen and soldiers, armed with swords and spears, javelins and sables, muskets and rifles; everyone followed Carl towards his rendezvous with fate and the battle for truth against evil.

Carl led his followers through lush lands of anemone and coltsfoot, crocus and bluebell, daisy and lady's slipper, shaded by elm and lime trees with the sunlight sifting through the leaves. But eventually they came to a desolate moor, a barren region of heather and holly and willow thickets and rose bushes, thorny things with small modest berries. This moorland was the assembly area he had deemed perfect for gathering his forces, and now he approached the place, seeing throngs of soldiers waiting in the no-time of The Land.

The waiting force was an innumerable historical expression of pike men, swordsmen, archers, lancers, marksmen and riflemen. One could see legionnaires with greaves, short swords and two spears, knights in chainmail, soldiers with bow and arrow, soldiers with muskets, soldiers with breech-loaders, and then scattered bands of adventurers, monks and dreamers with pitchforks, shot-guns, clubs and sticks, wearing iron pots and storm hats, and even early 20th century soldiers with Mauser Gewehr 98s, with pistols and sabres, having heard of the battle by word-of-mouth. It was indeed a motley crew but with a big heart in the right place: what was important for a recruit in this force was the will to fight for Light and life.

The clouds drifted by in the grey skies above roads paved with good intentions and Carl shouted a command to the forces, order-ing Eustace le Jeune to report to him. Eventually the knight rode forth, in his habitual blue livery dotted with golden fleurs-de-lis. When he had arrived Carl told him to arrange the formation of 'an open square'. When this was done, Carl rode into the centre of this U-shaped configuration, halted and delivered a speech to his crowd.

"Comrades, soldiers and warriors," began the Grey Knight. "We have gathered here in force but we haven't finished with our recruitment yet. My companion Ivan Ivanovich is currently riding in the mythical parts of The Land, gathering legendary warriors for our cause, heroes of myth and legend. I ask you to welcome them to our forces.

"Moreover, now I need to name a commander, a colonel for this army to act as my commander because, as you know, I have a personal mission beyond the battlefield. I shall participate with all vigour in the battle but my main aim is to proceed beyond here and to Hell as quickly as possible. Maybe we'll have to defeat the dark army before I can get to the gates of Hell beyond Gnipaheden, or maybe I can slip by during the battle by some ruse. Therefore, I hereby name you, Eustace le Jeune, as commander-in-chief of the army of the Light.

"You're in charge now," Carl told le Jeune as he approached him. "Now, we'll simply have to wait. When Ivan arrives with his throng we'll ride to Gnipaheden, the battlefield of destiny."

"Will do, sir," le Jeune said calmly, then adding in a thundering voice so that all of the units could hear him, "I hereby take command of the army of the Light."

Carl nodded and said quietly to his commander, "As for myself, I shall go and meditate nearby now."

He rode off alone, dismounted and sat down with a large stone at his back for support. He concentrated on the mantra "I am", as he had done even in the everyday world of Romania in 1917 and before, and even afterwards in The Land, being inspired in this by the Gospel of John in which Christ seven times says these words, such as "I am the light of the world."

This mantra is the answer to the riddle of existence. Life only started to exist when primaeval will met thought and chose the Light. And God, thus being created, said "I am".

CHAPTER SIXTEEN

IVAN'S RIDE

Meanwhile Ivan rode to diverse places in The Land in order to find promising recruits.

Ivan was a man of humble origins but he had a spark in the eye. This was his chief asset. He may have been a simple man yet no simpleton. Ivan sprang from the depths of the Russian rural population, the masses that recently had been serfs but from the 1860s onwards had lived more freely, a people by some deemed as uneducated; but Ivan was no illiterate *muzhik*, he had talent and potential. After elementary school he had been a furrier's apprentice in Moscow and during this time he had attended evening classes in Economics and Russian, enabling him to become an assistant bookkeeper.

Then war came, in August 1914, and the seventeen year-old Ivan was called up to serve in the cavalry. He trained as a trooper and then fought in various units in Masuria, Poland and East Prussia (later to be known as Memelland), rising from the rank of private to brevet sergeant with the promise of attending non-commissioned officers' school if conditions permitted. In the spring of 1917 he was transferred to the HQ of the Ivanovskich Cavalry Regiment where he became a NCO orderly, a team leader of despatch riders and staff helpers. And as such Carl spotted him and his worth.

Now it was much later and in another world. Ivan the common man with his indomitable spirit, the spark in his watery blue eyes and the easy smile in his moon-shaped face, a true-hearted smile that expressed 'everything will be all right', this Ivan now rode through The Land led by his intuition, projecting from his mind the ways he remembered from past adventures and the virtual ways he and Carl had taken.

Eventually, at some no-time, Ivan ended up on a plain with scattered groves of fir and cypress. It wasn't long before he saw a mountain in the distance. He saw Gremoburg, the free city on the mountain, its red and brown houses perched atop the boulders, crowning the greenish mountainside that basked in the afternoon sun.

"Here, perhaps, I'll find Krygon," Ivan said aloud to himself. "I remember how we talked with him when we first arrived at the city, this custodian and ruler of the place. With his violet clothes and confident countenance he seemed to be a good sword to have on your side."

Looking out over the plain below the hill, Ivan spotted a company, a unit of riders lead by a tall man wearing a tricorne hat. They rode down over the plain and into a cypress grove where they rested. At the saddles of some of the horses were hung game birds. Ivan slapped his horse and rode towards the company. He soon came before the entourage, the hunting party led by the man in the hat, all now sitting on the grass and refreshing themselves with wine.

"Greetings, men of honour! I'm Ivan Ivanovich Masov. I am a warrior of the Light, a fighter for truth and justice."

"Hail," said the hat man and stood up. "You seem familiar…"

"Well," said Ivan, "yes, I have been here before, with Carl Griffensteen, the Grey Knight, seeking spiritual information."

The man in the hat was indeed Krygon, his diamond-shaped face and serene countenance half-hidden below the brim. It was not a monk's calm, no, it was the warrior's calm he radiated – the tiger's calm, a restrained force always ready to act. He was, as always, perfectly dressed in violet as befitted a spirited warrior and pious ruler, his coat, jacket, breeches and boots all in different shades of violet, burgundy, purple and crimson.

"Ah, it's you," Krygon said, inspecting Ivan's grey uniform, Russian leather boots and M/16 cap, all attributes that he now recognised. "The pilgrims with swords!"

"That we were," agreed Ivan. "And when we parted, you said that we might come back and see you anytime."

"I did say that. So what brings you here?"

"A battle is brewing," Ivan said, "a battle against the forces of darkness. Devilry is gathering on Gnipaheden, attempting to alter and subdue our world. Indeed, the future of all of The Land and the omniverse is at stake. Will you come with me and fight for the Light, battle with me alongside Carl Griffensteen, my master and my companion on the journey, the Grey Knight?" Ivan may have been a sergeant and the son of a peasant, but he had his education and his resources, being able to find the right words when it was needed.

"This sounds like grave tidings," Krygon replied. "I would like to participate, but just wait for a moment." He went away into the copse and conferred with his men for a while before returning to Ivan. "Yes, we'll follow you, every one of us. We'll just take care of our prey and eat a little, then we shall ride to Gnipaheden."

They invited Ivan for a meal back in Gremoburg. Then they all rode off, Ivan directing the purple riders to the Five Roads junction, he himself continuing his mission to the City of Gold, the famed Tiramon, where a few old reclining warriors were tired of the rest and wanted to come out to cross swords again. Next it was on to Stegion, the City of Fools, and then to the Tao Land,

the eastern fairyland with its samurais and kshatriyas, the home
of Yoritomo and Shensi whom Ivan and Carl had once met in The
Land. For their part, Yoritomo and Shensi were certainly prepared
to assist him in his task, with a band of samurai and ashigaru,
swordsmen and musketeers. The word being spread in this Tao
World there soon banded together some other legendary names
like Arjuna, Lakshmi Bai, the Monkey King, Yoshitsune and Nitta
Yoshisada; these eastern legends also wanted to fight for light and
harmony against the Dark and confusion.

Next, Ivan's growing crowd was joined by figures from western
legends too, having heard about the battle threatening their neighbourhoods in The Land. The omniverse included all legendary
vistas, climes and story cycles so it was no surprise that the army
of the Light was filled eventually with volunteers like Tannhäuser,
Odysseus, the Nine Riders of Ostrogothia, Tommy Atkins, Harry
Hellfire, Aeneas, Sigurd Fafnesbane and many others. They were
fine fighters all, yet all offset by the dark side who had volunteers
like Hagen Gronje, Didrik Slagheck, Duryodhana and other nota-
ble men of infamous renown.

And so Ivan drummed up a large company. If it would be
enough, no-one could know. However, every man counted in the
impending struggle between good and evil, for light against darkness. It was lions and eagles against rats and crows.

Sitting by the stone in the assembly area, Carl saw an orderly
approach on horseback. The striker said that Ivan had arrived with
his cohorts so Carl then got up, mounted his steed and rode to
the centre of things. There he met Ivan himself with whom he
exchanged a few words. The gist of it was that everything was now
ready for the battle. Ivan had also recruited legendary fighters
from myth and saga, from The Land and from beyond the Beyond.

Le Jeune, the acting commander, had already been informed. So now he gave the orders to move forward; the army broke camp and marched to Gnipaheden. A cornet in le Jeune's wake carried the army flag, a white cloth with a green-lined golden cross.

The army of the Dark knew that their opponents were gathering and therefore they had deployed on the farthest part of Gnipaheden, blocking the way to the Tree of Evil. The army of the Light pulled up in a corresponding array on the proximal side of the plain with the cavalry on the wings and infantry in the centre. Le Jeune planted his banner in the joint behind the right wing and the middle part of the army. Along with the golden cross standard, the new army sported variegated banners with inspiring heraldry such as castles, wreaths, swords, unicorns and egrets. Everything was ready for the battle.

From the opposite ranks now emanated two riders. One of them was dressed in black breeches, black fur jacket and riding boots and, on the head, a busby with the Death's Head Hussar emblem. The other man wore a dark tunic and harem pants, and a cloak with the hood up. Carl made a reassuring gesture towards le Jeune, called Ivan over, put his heels into the flanks of his horse and with his squire rode slowly out to meet the sombre riders. The clouds scudded across the sky, dramatic clouds tumbling along and over each other in silver-grey, blue-grey and blue-grey-blue swirls. A crow cawed in the distance but otherwise all was quiet save for the faint jingling, stomping and hawking from innumerable men and horses, waiting in battle order.

The dark riders had already reached a place in the middle of the field, right between the two armies. The hussar put a monocle to his eye and nodded towards Carl and Ivan. Carl recognised the man immediately for his nutcracker face with its elongated features and ruddy cheeks.

"So, we meet again," said Carl when he halted before the man whom he had last met at Castle Munte.

"Indeed, we do," said Körner. "Carl Griffensteen, it's an honour."

"The same, Maximilian Körner."

The clouds drifted silently, ominously by. The crow cawed again. Otherwise there was only the sound of horses snorting, hooves stomping, war horses of both armies being nervous before the battle.

"Now let me introduce my master," Körner said. "I present to you, Morven." The other man put down the hood, baring his bald head and his impassioned face with its pained smile.

"Morven," Carl said, unperturbed. "I enjoyed my last stay with you very much."

"Thank you," said Morven and continued to smile. "Such a shame that we can't do the same now, spending time drinking and talking."

"It seems not. A battle is brewing, eh?"

"It seems so. When I understood what you were doing in The Land, what your mission meant, then I couldn't sit idly by."

"So you drummed up this handy little rabble?"

"Actually, Körner did that. Well, on my inspiration, that's true. But the execution of it was all of Körner's doing. He has so many contacts with all the dark elements of this world and the past and the next."

"But you, yes both of you," Carl said, "are trying to stop me in my mission. So tell me, what's wrong with trying to redeem the Devil?"

"Surely you understand?" said Morven, with a slight sarcastic laugh. "Because if you succeed, everything becomes pointless. It would spell the end of our tormenting and haunting people, of concocting devilry and perverting innocence, corrupting the sacred and getting the holy to sell itself for a pot of stew. All the things that we live for. Yes, and even more than that, the very linchpin, the very ground stopper of the world will go out. There is the risk of everything returning to Logos – including you, my good Captain. Have you thought of that?

"Earth will be dissolved and all things, all beings, all the flowers and animals and humans will return to the astral abode where they first emerged as archetypes. Is that what you want? Do you want the Earth to be dematerialised, to bring on the eschaton? Are you ready for it, soldier? Are you really done living your lives as a soldier, done living in the earthly dimension? Are you done with your adventures in the storybook world and the real world? Have you partied for the last time, are you done wining and dining and having your witty conversations? Have you kissed a beautiful woman for the last time, and are you done admiring the clouds on a summer's day?"

Taken aback, Carl considered this for a moment. Would all of the world, this and the other dimensions of the omniverse, really disappear if he redeemed Yaldabaoth? It sounded plausible the way Morven spoke. But he couldn't actually ponder this in a normal, discursive way, finding himself for the moment in something of an altered state, in an operational trance. The mission was drawing to a close and he must pursue it, even if the world was dissolved, even if Earth too was 'redeemed' in the process, becoming a celestial neighbourhood with minstrel song into eternity, a subtle sphere free of sensuality with all that would imply.

He studied his counterpart, noting the red lining of Morven's cloak. He had style, this you have to admit, Carl thought. But how did Morven's sermon compare to Pelagion's story – didn't he say that the world was the asuras' creation? This in itself beautiful world had asurean origin yet it was populated with tangible copies of astral models made by God. The world was a material mirror of heavenly lands. So this meant…

Carl looked towards the dark army with its banners and pennants waving in the wind. Their leaders also had some style. Just too bad their hordes were so disgusting, with their worship of rats and atrophy, of darkness and suffering.

CHAPTER SEVENTEEN
GNIPAHEDEN

So this was the parley before the battle, the mounted group of Carl, Ivan, Körner and Morven occupying a spot half-way between the two armies deployed on Gnipaheden. As for Morven's argument, Carl had made up his mind – or so he thought – for the man's enticing rhetoric had little effect on him.

"True," he responded, "I like to admire the clouds on a summer day. But it's not summer here, not here and now, and I can see black clouds ahead. I'm surrounded by stony ground and barrenness. Yes, by the way, probably the world is in some way Yaldabaoth's creation, and Pelagion himself told me that. But what's in it of goodness and light, this has come there through God's wishes and the devas' actions. So *fiat justitia, et pereat mundus.*"[3]

Morven paled a tad.

"Now there's no turning back," Carl continued. "I'm going to Sheol and to redeem Yaldabaoth and you are standing in my way. So back off or I'll let the weapons speak to you."

Morven lowered his brow to appear thoughtful, now trying to

---

[3] "Let the world perish as long as justice prevails." (Johannes Manlius, 1563) The phrase was famously quoted by Ferdinand I, Holy Roman Emperor, and later by Immanuel Kant.

present his case in a more conciliatory vein.

"You don't say. But –"

"You can't tempt me," Carl interjected.

"I can't?" Morven still tried again. "But what about the pos-sibility of you coming into our service? We have opportunities, you know, and great resources. Never mind the so-called darkness that you seem programmed to dislike, think instead of the wealth, the opportunities and power that could be yours! Think of the kingdoms and the armies, the chance to reshape Earth's ways… you can become a legend, you can become history's greatest man, whether this be in The Land or in our own world or any world in the omniverse that you choose."

Carl was amused by what Morven said so he stayed silent and let him continue.

"So, my friend, my dear Carl, I can offer you the command of our army, for example. It's an invincible corps, representing all the lust for power and all the jingoism and all the pride that has ever existed. With you at its head we can take it for a victorious ride through The Land and all of the omniverse, making everywhere a playground for your will, your ideas and your desires!"

In two minds now, Carl listened to the other's speech. Somewhere inside his mind, part of him began to be attracted, no doubt about it. It would indeed be interesting to become a legendary hero, to fashion The Land according to his ideas and to recreate history and myth after his own measure. Sure, he wanted to fight for the Light but sometimes you could be drawn to another, easier life, a more simple and tangible one. He had not always been faithful, had not always been a Bible-reading esotericist. Even Carl had his moments of weakness, even he could falter. Was this, then, about to happen here at Gnipaheden?

"You can become a ruler of the ethereal worlds," Morven said next, sensing his opportunity growing, "and fashion it in your own image. You can let your will be projected onto space-time and shape it by your own thoughts. You can be a city builder, for example. You would not even need to be cruel in the process, there'd be no need for any murder and fire regime. You could build cities with palaces and temples of marble and gold, porphyry and malachite…" He let the idea hang in the air for a moment.

"My own cities?" mused Carl. "That might be fun, to be an architect, a builder of cities. I do have some ideas about that."

"Yes," said Morven quickly, "and I can realise them, becoming your executive arm. And when the palaces are built you can have feasts and fancy balls – you can gather around you your own harem with every conceivable favourite. And you can build theatres and organise hunts and expeditions…"

When Morven mentioned 'harem' Carl suddenly came back to himself, realising that this all began to resemble bidding tactics from the other side. He needed, for example, no harem; he just wanted to see his Greensleeves again. He didn't say that openly.

"It seems to me," he said instead, "you've gone too far, sugaring your offer way too much."

"Really? But surely –"

"Yes, you have," Carl said. "For example, I need no fancy dinners. I'm a soldier and I eat well enough anyway. I can't eat more than my fill."

"Yet –"

"So there you have it. And I don't need to be historical, a legend, for I am that already. I'm the Grey Knight, known throughout The Land and the omniverse, throughout all of history. I'm part of history, just by living and fighting and riding in these grey rags and thus creating a legend of it all. And in case you were wondering, I don't need to command the world's largest army, for having been a captain in the Russian Army is good enough. There's nothing more intense than being the leader of men, fighting in a cavalry company in a modern war. And beyond that, moreover, consider this very army of the Light set before you with my commander

Eustace le Jeune at its head – do you not think I already have a rather important position? I am the one who has recruited and unified this army, and my position as standard-bearer is recognised by all. And I fully enjoy that, win or lose."

"Yeah, yeah –" tried Morven, but Carl wasn't finished yet.

"I don't need your princely pleasures, I don't need theatres and harems and adventures. Recently, in The Land, I've pretty much had my fill of adventures. And as for pleasures, I amuse myself rather well with a good book."

That said, Carl certainly did want to live in a world of adventure; this he had dreamed of before encountering the somewhat ghastly, grisly, muddy battles of the World War. Before his arrival in The Land he had dreamed of a world where one might seek treasures and discover new countries, an infinite world of fairytales and adventures. Oddly, now that he knew The Land and all it meant, this kind of adolescent adventure didn't attract him anymore, not when he had a mission from Heaven to complete. But aside from that, was "a good book" enough to amuse him? In a way, yes, for his will was in command of his being.

"I see," murmured Morven and smiled sardonically. He realised that Carl couldn't be enticed with goods and gold, power and strength, so then he tried another strategy to undermine his foe. "You say you don't need me and what I have to offer, being content with what you have, it seems. So you can't be moved, being such a devout man. But if you're so pious, then why do you refer to your service as a captain, or to the legend of the Grey Knight, as if to show how good you are?"

"What do you mean?" asked Carl.

"A pious man is, surely, simply pious. He is satisfied with nothing, satisfied with the sky above and the ground below him, with a bed and a roof over his head. So what are all these grand words about your rank and your supposed mission? Not exactly humble, I'd say.

"And what if it were all put to the test?" he continued with cunning. "Let's say you did escape past us, come to Sheol and there redeem Yaldabaoth and then return to your world. And once there you found that everyone ignored it all, that evil lived on as before with people's usual desires having their run, with murder and debauchery continuing to exist – for people do not easily give up their pleasures. And you, my good Carl Griffensteen, are shunted out of the army you served in because it ceases to exist, and you must go home to your native land where you become an outcast, a senile fool who says he met with the Devil and prayed for him, yet no-one believes you!"

"But –" Carl interposed, but now it was Morven who was in command of the argument.

"Let's say you become an oddball, a tramp, a beggar. Would you then still be happy with your life and all you thought you had achieved, still rejoicing with piety over what you had? A bowl of soup every other day, a glove you can find on the street. True joy, eh? No, more than likely you'd be depressed and you'd start seeing everything in black. A character like you would become obsessive and begin to torment yourself with feelings of inadequacy. Every thought, every breath would become a self-inflicted pain.

"But all of this you would still enjoy because you're devout, because you have your faith? The whole thing is just a spiritual challenge for the godly man, right, and so you rename yourself Job? So there you have your faith, my pious Grey Knight, the true legend. This is what your beliefs tell you to think, that to strive for goods and gold is just vanity and true joy is just to breathe the air. That's what you zealots declare, isn't it? A life of poverty and dirt is of no matter, a life of obsessive thoughts and depression are just self-inflicted and your faith will fix everything!"

Carl hesitated. What Morven said had hit a nerve and he needed time to consider this. So he asked another question first, to soften his opponent.

"Depression and obsession aside, let's look instead at the other side. Do you mean to say that I would be safe in the service of darkness? I wouldn't still be rejected and have to become a beggar anyway?"

"That is precisely what I am saying. With us you are safe, with us you have a position. Never mind about being a general or conquering the world, then, you get a high position in any case. For example this – you are in The Land now, this adventurous fairyland, so wouldn't you like to live here forever? You can be an adventurous captain with service in The Land or in your world or wherever you want, to come and go as you please in time and space, throughout the wonders of the omniverse! You could see impossible lands and cross swords with strange beings, find treasures and rescue kidnapped virgins, see palaces and temples, cross the oceans in stupendous ships, ride across deserts and through jungles in search of indescribable monsters… You can search through enigmatic maps in dusty libraries, roam through a white city in search of the wise man who has the key to ancient secrets, venture through rustling forests in search of the troll who guards a priceless pearl and fight with the troll to return triumphantly with the pearl to a king you promised to fetch it for? How about it, Captain?

"And when you've had enough of adventure, then you'll receive a home from us, a cosy little cottage or a resplendent villa, whatever you choose, where you get to live like a monk if you want to. You can live the life of a hermit with classic books and a garden and peace and quiet, or even live with a lady friend that we surely can find for you. You can have all this. You only need bow to the power of the Dark, to the black boot and the rat banner, to Yaldabaoth and to me!"

Now this sounded different, Carl thought. One could serve darkness even as an adventurer, maybe riding around in this land forever with adventure every day, good dining and sleeping under the stars. And when he got tired of it all he'd have a guaranteed retreat, a heart-warming abode with a rich library... and all he had to do was to switch sides and give allegiance to the dark banner. There would be no threat of an insecure future, of a desolate life in a poor Finland, his homeland, where Morven suggested that he would end up desolate if he chose the narrow path.

Carl must choose now, to fight for the Light or to switch sides in order to become a leisurely adventurer, or whatever. True, he also liked the adventure of fighting for the Light, and in the long run to complete the mission entrusted to him, to get to Sheol. But even then, as Morven pictured it, the intercessory mission might result in no essential change having been achieved, with the people of the world ignoring it, lacking the will to realise it and as usual inclined to desire and craving, lust and strife. And what if he had no place in the world, if he faced the fate of becoming a beggar and an outcast? Then to choose the life of an adventurer in The Land would surely be more enticing. Even to complete this assignment in Sheol but then just go on to an uncertain future, this was something of a gamble.

He must therefore choose between the one and the other. He must mobilise his free will. It was simple – but the simple was difficult, as the Prussian General Carl von Clausewitz had said. He breathed out, trying to find peace as he sat in the saddle at Gnipaheden, sitting in front of his adversary Morven on his own steed.

Carl tried to find himself in the moment, to find the power of the present.

And he did so, thus the choice was made by itself. He didn't deliberate formally, didn't put up mental columns of 'for' and 'against', no, he only fostered his will. And will chose itself, it chose the Light. In that very moment, Carl began to smile 'the smile of the liberated'.

Morven had truly afflicted him with enticing visions, tempting him with a life as a free adventurer in The Land, and Carl just smiled at this because he realised that if this was what the darkness had to offer then it was powerless; it had nothing to put up against a man with a free will. The very nature of will is to be free. And a man's freedom is to realise his own limitations and to be secure in his essence, to find calm in his inner mind, whether as beggar or king.

By summoning his will, Carl defeated the darkness within himself. He defeated all the things that Morven had tried to ensnare him with, even 'fine' things such as the life of an adventurer in strange lands with a guaranteed pension in the form of a hermit cottage with its garden and library. Given that this also required him to bow to Morven and the Dark, it wouldn't be a life worthy of the name. Carl simply rejected it. He defeated the darkness within himself. He wasn't afraid to continue his mission, even if it was to be pointless in the long run, even if it did lead to a life of poverty for him personally. If he ended up in such an existence, he would, he told himself, still make it into the best life possible by using his will, his free will.

Carl smiled triumphantly and Morven realised that he had lost.

"You can offer what you want," was Carl's response, "riches and countries and thrones and slaves or the simple life as an adventurer in The Land. It doesn't matter, any of it. The most valuable thing we own is the tranquility within ourselves. All I want is to live in light and freedom, be it as a beggar or a tramp, an officer or whatever else. Nothing of what the good man really wants can be found in darkness and materialism. Ultimately, the Dark is just emptiness and meaninglessness, anxiety and fear, chaos and confusion."

"Although –" But Morven had nothing to add and he knew it, he just felt that he had to say something for the sake of it.

"Sorry, my friend," Carl said, with a touch of sarcasm himself for once, "the culmination has already been reached, reached and passed. True, I wavered for a moment but then I found myself, I found my willpower again. I found balance, composure and control. I found peace and quiet, light and life within me. And thus I defeated my darkness."

"And I am defeated in this argument, perhaps," muttered Morven with little grace. "But now our battle remains, we shall still have to fight. You must defeat my army of the Dark to get to Sheol."

"Indeed I must," Carl said. "May the best side win."

Morven nodded and turned his horse as Körner touched his fur cap to Carl and then followed his master to their own side. Carl and Ivan watched them ride away and then did the same, turning to ride back to their own soldiers.

CHAPTER EIGHTEEN
THE BATTLE

The two armies faced one another. The clouds went by, nothing happened. There was a silence for a few minutes. Then, with a sign from Körner, cow horns and elephant horns were raised and blown, and ratchets and bird pipes joined in the commotion. On the other side, bronze horns and silver horns were raised and blown, singing out their vibrant notes. The forces started to advance.

Le Jeune's plan was first to let the cavalry attack and then let the infantry take advantage of the chaos created in this way. Mounted archers rode in the lead and fired their volleys, the salvo contained by the enemy, catching the arrows on their shields. Then shiny, heavy cavalry thundered in among the dark hordes with felled lances and closed visors. Some of them were pulled down and killed while others rode out through the storm and returned to attack again and again.

After this the infantry was sent in to exploit the disorder, steady men in green, red and yellow liveries, in legionnaires' armour and 1800s' blues and many other outfits, advancing with spear and bardisan, sword and sabre, pallasch and naginata. They clashed with the other side's dagger men, swordsmen and spear fighters. Death's Head Hussars assaulted the flanks of the light forces at the same time as knights in black cross-liveries attacked them at the back. Then the Nine Riders of Ostrogothia effected a cavalry shock and scattered the Death's Head warriors, denying the riders of the black cross a foothold.

In co-operation with le Jeune, Carl rode behind the infantry line commanding the troops. There was no point in riding at the head, he knew. His mission came first, although he was certainly ready to fight and fall here if needed. Ivan rode as bodyguard beside him, ready to protect his life with his sabre, his revolver and his happy mood.

On this plain of Gnipaheden, fringed by low mountains under a red sky, they fought. The battle surged back and forth, with giving and taking, with life and death, the Light against the Dark. It was a struggle between a future of flowers and birdsong and one of gnawing rats, of green meadows and of sterile soils. It was between responsibility and nihilism. It was between the friendly, caring hand and the boot stamping on a human face. Forever.

The battle raged on in a state of timelessness. It was infantry against cavalry, infantry against infantry, cavalry against cavalry, while above them all in the sky veritable steel birds attacked, mechanical birds of prey created by Bestos Fokalion, the mad engineer whom Körner once had hired to attack Carl and Ivan. Now a new generation of Bestos' steel monsters was ready to fight. They circled over the fateful Gnipaheden, at a given moment making an orchestrated nosedive towards the army of the Light. One or another of them reached its goal and infested its prey, drawing blood with its steel claws. Others became the victims of a particular group of riflemen whom Carl had recruited, a unit of Swedes from the mid-1800s, fellows uniformed in dark blue, with caps on their heads and belts with cartridge pockets, armed with the needle-fire *zündnadelgewehr*. Their 8 mm projectiles hit the steel birds and made them plunge into piles of scrap iron.

It was army against army, battalion against battalion, company against company. But then gradually the fighting became disorganised and chaotic. There were scuffles of groups and there were duels man-to-man. Sigurd Fafnesbane dueled with Duryodhana, Odysseus crossed swords with Ganelon, Yoshitsune engaged Cronstedt. Hagen Gronje and Didrik Slagheck tried to defeat Tannhäuser together but Tommy Atkins and Harry Hellfire came to the rescue.

Everything became confused. This was not a strategic affair any longer, not a battle one could lead but more like a mass duel. Good and evil were hopelessly entangled, and it was every man for himself. The two armies fought one another, two exuberant entities each trying to overwhelm the other, trying to gain inroads to the other as water penetrates relative to the resistance offered to it. The commotion was difficult to grasp, impossible to fathom if one were involved. But on each side the respective commander had a kind of overview, Eustace le Jeune on the side of the Light, Maximilian Körner on the other side. Neither of them would give up the task of battle command, and they both sent out and received orderlies to find out what was happening.

The reliable Ivan Ivanovich was still with Carl, alive and fighting, keeping himself close to the Grey Knight; still mounted, they now fought Pappenheimers with their sabres.

"Fierce fighting!" Ivan said, breathing heavily.

"Indeed," said Carl. "But we're fighting for a just cause, a good cause. And if we see it through, maybe the world will be saved forever." And in his mind, Carl heard the most famous words of von Clausewitz: "Pursue one great decisive aim with force and determination."

He also remembered Morven's words, that the whole world might return to a spiritual state if the mission succeeded, that "the very linchpin... of the world will go out." Everything then would return to God in its original form, the Thought and Will of the primordial state, the Logos. A dematerialisation bringing on the eschaton. But Carl didn't believe this. In order for this to happen, each and every human being would have to intend it and there were certainly no signs in the world of every man and woman suddenly becoming pious. The Earth was created by mistake, as Pelagion had intimated, being an asurean creation from beginning to end including all humans and animals, the model for all living things being nonetheless eternal and divine.

Then again, Carl thought, you never knew. Maybe Heaven on Earth was indeed imminent.

"From Logos we come, to Logos we shall return," Carl screamed as he brought down a dark rider with a thrust to the heart. The next moment, Carl looked away into the distance and he seemed to see all worlds at once, including this one, the everyday world he came from; and even there he saw the battle raging, not only in the current World War but in all wars from time immemorial to now and, verily, even into all possible futures. Everything was depending on this moment, everything flowed together in this battle and this mission to find Yaldabaoth and pray for him. Surely that would stop the war, not only this war but war as a phenomenon, all wars past, present and future? A war to end all wars?

Captain Carl Griffensteen reached for the water bottle that hung at his saddle and as he drank he suddenly saw open land behind him, unoccupied by the enemy. In fact, something very strange had happened: when the armies had clinched, each side had tried to bypass the other's left flank with the result that the fronts had turned 180 degrees. And this meant that the path to Hell was now open. The Evil Tree, to which the enemy had blocked the path with his line, was now to the back of the army of Light. This would allow Carl to ride through and away on his mission, perhaps to complete his quest. He had a home run.

Carl cried out to Ivan, gesturing towards the open country at the back. His squire nodded. The pair rode off along the line and eventually found the command post of le Jeune, the place marked by the white banner with a golden cross planted beside it.

"Hold the lines there!" Carl said to his mounted acting commander. "We're making a little excursion. My goal is in sight and, God willing, the mission will soon be over. In short, I'm away to the Evil Tree and to Hell."

"God bless you indeed!" le Jeune called back. "We'll keep the battle going, staving off the forces of evil. We'll hold them where they are and stand or fall."

With the din of battle ringing in their ears, Carl and Ivan rode away fast from the battlefield, over naked rock, over shingle and sand, across eastern Gnipaheden and towards their destination in the distance. The dense, dark clouds incessantly tumbled by above their heads, yet not a blade of grass was seen and of water there was none.

"A country of stone," observed Ivan.

"Undeniably," the knight agreed.

Strong winds blew as they galloped across the wasteland. Behind them, at Gnipaheden, the battle raged, the affair undecided, so there was still the risk of the Light being defeated by the Dark and the remnants of that vicious army setting out after them. The landscape was desolate, flat and monotonous, and they seemed to be riding for a long time. But then suddenly, in the middle of the plain ahead, there appeared one single thing, a large tree with contorted shapes and sporting sickly flowers in red and blue. The tree top lost itself in the upper layers of the atmosphere.

"Is it…?"

"Yes, this has to be the Evil Tree, springing from the root of all evil," said Carl, with Parysatis' words in his mind.

"What shall we do with the horses?"

"We must trust that God will take care of them," the knight said.

He rode up, dismounted and began to examine the tree, the one through which they might reach Sheol. It was a broad and ancient tree, and hollow with an entrance just large enough for a man. The two men, having entered the trunk, found in the interior a staircase leading upward. Fearlessly and without delay they began to ascend it, the steps turning tortuously in a spiral, up and up. Soon they had lost count of the steps. Then without warning everything became white and hazy and they found themselves in a new, unfamiliar neighbourhood with sparsely growing trees and bordered by strange rocks in the distance. Everything was veiled by a cold, grey-blue mist. Ivan asked if this could really be Hell.

"Probably," replied his master. "Let's go out and see what we can find."

"But we're here to find Yaldabaoth, right?"

"That's the one. Lucifer. The Prince of Darkness. The Devil himself."

They set off warily across the landscape and eventually a coastal area became visible. Ivan and Carl found themselves standing on a crag, peering out over a misty sea.

"This place scares me," said Ivan.

"Maybe that's how it should be. It would be a lot worse if you loved it," replied the knight.

"You're probably right."

They descended the rock and walked along the coast for a while, along the stony, dark sand beach of the foggy main. They said nothing but Carl for his part was in comparatively good spirits since they had already come so far. Before long they noticed something out there on the waves, the outline of a craft approaching the beach. They stood still and waited. When the hull emerged from the fog, the sight surprised them for the ship was completely built of bones, of ribs, scapulae and crania. Neither of them said anything, they just waited. Presently there appeared on deck a man in a beret and a kaftan, a vivid and awe-inspiring figure with a long beard and open countenance.

"Greetings, adventurers," he shouted. "I'm Gomer Staak. I can take you to Sheol City."

"Really?" Carl called back, introducing himself and his companion. "Then we'll come aboard if you'll have us."

A rope ladder was lowered and a dinghy launched, rowed by an aide to Staak, a taciturn, hunchbacked figure. When the craft arrived at the shore the two soldiers stepped aboard and were rowed out to the ship. There they climbed the bony steps of the ladder and soon found themselves standing on a deck of bones, joints and skulls.

"Good of you to take us to our goal," said Carl.

"Well," said Staak, "I felt that something important was afoot. Or, to be honest, an angel told me that you were coming."

Aha, Carl thought, a little angelic guidance even here at the end. Beautiful. Pelagion was still around, watching over things.

"So bring us to our goal, please," Carl said.

"Of course. But first I have to have the Rose. It's the ticket."

"What?" said Carl, taken aback.

"The Rose That Never Fades. I think you know the one. It's the ticket for this trip to central Sheol."

"Ah, I see," said the knight, groping inside his tunic and taking out the golden flower he had safely carried so far. Staak took it, stuck it unceremoniously in his beret and shouted an order to his one sailor, the hunchback. Carl and Ivan took themselves off to some bony deck chairs and sitting on these they were transferred over the Sea of Hell to Sheol City, where they hoped to find Yaldabaoth.

They journeyed who knows how long across the leaden grey, misty ocean expanse until at last they saw a coastline in the distance, steeped in pale light from a distant sun. Some chains from the beach, Staak ordered the hunchback to lower the dinghy into the sea and soon the soldiers were rowed ashore, having to wade the last part through shallow water. The hunchback returned to the ship. Standing on the beach, the pair waved to the skipper who waved back cheerfully and disappeared into the fog with his vessel.

Where to go now in this new part of Hell, to reach Sheol City? As if in a trance, Carl walked out across the barren neighbourhood with Ivan walking silently, faithfully by his side. They followed intuition.

'And so what shall I do now?' Carl thought. 'I must simply find Yaldabaoth and pray for him, this Yaldabaoth, the Devil, Lucifer, the Prince of Darkness? Something like that.' The walk gave Carl time to remember the internal reserves of goodness he indeed could evoke, and the moment when at the inn he had realised that it was he himself who must do it, that it was he himself who was the good man the angel had bade him find. He also remembered how he had resisted the temptations of Morven at Gnipaheden, how he had willingly chosen to continue the mission that now, it seemed, was about to reach its end.

CHAPTER NINETEEN
TOWARDS THE GOAL

They caught sight of the silhouette of a city in the distance. It was Sheol City and even from afar they could make out its ruins and misty remnants, pathetic symbols of fallen glory.

Walking on, they came to a main road and followed it to the city centre. There, in a square, they saw a baroque building, a grand and strange artefact in black sandstone with a roofline adorned by gargoyles. The building radiated spiritual power, but of a devious kind. One's gaze lost itself in its arcades and fronts but the wide stairway seemed inviting.

"What could this be?" Ivan wondered. "Yaldabaoth's house, do you think?"

"I don't know. Let's have a look."

Solemnly, they went up the steps, slipped into a gallery and found a passageway to the interior of the building. Everything was of enormous proportions and all was strange and elaborate: draperies, forgotten objects from asurean machinations, trophies from the war against Heaven and *objets d'art* that asuras had manufactured, all to pass the time in the Sheolian non-existence. At length they came to a hall, its dimensions huge and its corners somehow lost in obscurity. There was a kind of table in the middle of the hall, a catafalque of astral marble. Carl had an inspiration.

"I believe this building is the House of Demiourgos. The asuras would have created Man here. They must have experimented, engineering genes and forms until eventually they produced a likeness of themselves – man, that is, Adam. That's what we were told in Ghislane."

"Really?" Ivan asked, looking around wide-eyed. "So it all started here? It makes you wonder."

It was a fascinating place but they weren't here for sightseeing, they were looking for Yaldabaoth.

Sheol City was an impressive creation, for all its ruins. Its urban spaces were certainly not of this world. Ivan and Carl walked past palaces with black, grey and dark silver walls, they passed by large puddles and piles of broken rock, hearing echoes of bygone grandeur. They saw more grand buildings and artefacts, including a three-aisled building adorned by carnelian and agate. They decided to investigate this house. By way of a gallery and a dark vestibule they came to an auditorium with benches. The walls were of obsidian, the benches were of marble and the floor of red granite. This was Symposion, the parliament house of the asuras.

"This seems another familiar environment," Ivan said. "They would have sat here conferring, the demons, if one is to believe Pelagion."

"Pelagion? Yes, he told us about this," Carl agreed, sitting down on a white marble bench.

"But where do we find Yaldabaoth?"

"I have no idea," Carl said, "but we'll continue our search, wandering around in this Hell until we find him."

They rested on the benches for a while. Then they got back to their feet, out into the foggy daylight and walking around among the mists and vapours, the ruins and the decay. After a while they left the city itself behind them and came to a suburb of villas and detached houses. Finally they approached a beach house made of dark glass. They couldn't know it, but this was Yaldabaoth's summer house.

"How deserted all this is," Carl said, rather mystified. "Not even a few minor asuras seem to be around."

"Maybe the asuras left the place voluntarily," suggested Ivan, "gone to more heavenly climes. Do you think they've all repented and returned to their grandfather's house?"

"Maybe so," Carl said, remembering what Parysatis had said in Hortalion, something about asuras having turned from darkness to the Light.

They went into the glass house and roamed through the chambers. All were empty. No-one was there. They merely found shadowy, abstract paintings, half-empty bookshelves and cabinets with bizarre sculptures and figurines sitting on them. Passing through the house, they came to a terrace overlooking the misty sea. And here, sitting in the corner overlooking it all, they found a melancholy figure wearing a dark cape, a man, apparently, with well-groomed, curly hair and a curious expression in an indescribable face.

"Yaldabaoth, I presume?" asked Carl, bowing slightly.

The figure nodded and said, "Yes, I'm Yaldabaoth."

Carl savoured the moment.

"And you are?" the other asked.

"I'm Carl Griffensteen, a man from Earth, here exploring Sheol. I wanted to come here and I wanted to see you."

"Indeed?" Yaldabaoth said, wrapping his cloak around himself.

"Yes," said Carl. "May I sit down with you? I'm just a man, a creature of the Light, like you. We all have the eternal Light within, don't we?"

"Possibly," Yaldabaoth said absently, continuing to look listlessly out over the main. He didn't seem surprised to receive visitors, nor interested.

The two soldiers found some chairs on the terrace and sat down a little distance away from Yaldabaoth. Carl knew that he must tread softly here or else the other might turn against him.

"On a day like this," Carl began, on the spur of the moment, "I come to think about my life, my early life in Finland as a boy, standing and looking up at the scudding clouds, little white clouds flying over the wide expanse of pine forest. The sun shone on me then and it has shone on me ever afterwards. I've also been in much darker climes. I've seen death and destruction. But the guidance of the inner light has never left me, there's always been some kind of internal lamp guiding me. Haven't you felt that, Yaldabaoth? Haven't you also recognised your inner light sometimes?"

"I might have," Yaldabaoth said, turning towards the men for the first time. "So you're from the Earth kingdom, the material world, eh? And now you're here. To see me. Strange. That hasn't happened in a long time."

"Indeed, I'm here to visit you, to see how you are. So how are things going for you? Do you have anything to while away the time with? Or does it get lonely?"

"I wouldn't say I'm lonely. But yes, it's a bit tedious here at times."

"I guess the grey weather must get to you," Carl tried. "Wouldn't you like some sun to shine on you?"

"But how do you suggest I do that? Pray to God, I suppose?"

"Well, yes, maybe," Carl replied, seizing the moment and putting his hands together in prayer. "Something like this. 'Dear God, send Your light to Sheol, to shine over its fields and ruins and endless vistas, to shine over this glass house and Your son, Yaldabaoth.'

"I, Carl Griffensteen, should like that. I wish for Yaldabaoth to have the sun shining over him, warming him. Because truly this Yaldabaoth is my brother, who has the same inner light as I do. I cannot endorse Yaldabaoth's deeds in the past, I cannot endorse the devilry, the darkness and black magic, the machinations and the plots that lead man astray. I want these acts of darkness to be a thing of the past. But on behalf of mankind I hereby forgive Yaldabaoth, the Prince of Darkness."

Carl had come to the core of his mission, to pray for Yaldabaoth and to draw the Light to him. Only then could he be redeemed, Pelagion had said, only by a man praying for Yaldabaoth and showing that he cared for him, this on behalf of mankind whom he, Yaldabaoth, had led away from the Light. And there was no turning back now, Carl realised, he just had to keep going. He saw that Yaldabaoth still sat in his chair, looking despondently at him, the prayerful knight in his own chair nearby. The foundation having been laid by his prayer, Carl now leaned forward and continued to focus on his task.

"I acknowledge the Light within him, the essence of good nature within Yaldabaoth which is the Light of God, the source of all light. With my will I bid light and love to flow here and unite in order to help this creature, Yaldabaoth, to leave the realms of evil and start to embrace the goodness within him."

Carl was interceding for Yaldabaoth, praying for the Prince of Darkness.

"But… what…?" Yaldabaoth stuttered, for he had never experienced anything like this before. Carl for his part continued to pray, letting the cosmic light flow out from within him, the divine spark of life we all have within us, the soul spark being a mirror of God's Light. The light of the human and the divine were thus united, becoming a wave of reality that washed over the terrace and the three of them, over Sheol and the whole world, The Land and all dimensions of the omniverse and through the Seven Heavens.

The most wonderful things then happened. Light shone through the dense clouds of the sky and the Sheol beach was suddenly lit up by an astral sun. And at this very moment a brightly shining assembly came down through the skies, the deva Hiranya and a great heavenly host, led there by virtue of Carl's intercession. Hiranya's entourage touched down on the shore and the shining devas stayed in the background to watch as the leader strode towards the glass house and its terrace where Carl, Ivan and Yaldabaoth sat. Carl now stood up, straightened and looked at the being dressed in a golden robe with a light blue surcoat. He had long hair and a mild countenance.

"I am Hiranya, leader of the devas. Greetings, Carl Griffensteen."

"Greetings," Carl said, bowing. The deva nodded to him.

"I thank you, Carl, for having prayed for another's salvation, praying for your brother Yaldabaoth to realise his inner light."

At the same moment, Yaldabaoth also got up from his chair and just stood there in silence before turning, seemingly about to leave. Hiranya now addressed him.

"Brother, why are you going? I've been led by this man's prayer, coming here to give you light, to bring you peace of mind after all this time."

"But no-one can enlighten me," said Yaldabaoth, defiantly. "In any case, every being must be angry with me. And even if I did approach God, He would throw me out of the cosmos, throw me away into emptiness like some wayward Prometheus to be forever gnawed by eagles."

"No," said Hiranya, "no-one can be thrown out of being. *Kein Wesen kann zu Nichts zerfallen.*[4] God's love will lead you to the Light."

"But what about the people?" Yaldabaoth argued, still resisting. "They all certainly hate me."

Hiranya then cast a glance at Carl, the Grey Knight, bareheaded and with a peaceful expression on his face. Entranced, Carl looked back at the deva, savouring the tranquility and solemnity of the moment.

"This son of Adam," Hiranya told Yaldabaoth, pointing towards Carl, "has prayed for you. On behalf of mankind he has forgiven you. And by this intercession, I have been led here to take you home. He is the symbol of mankind being ready to forgive you."

---

[4] "No being can dissolve to nothing." (Johann von Goethe, 1829)

Yaldabaoth was softened by these words.

"My brother, I see that you speak the truth. Your words and the man's intercession has brought out remorse in me." There was a long silence, heavy with feeling, while he considered his words. "Therefore…," he continued hesitantly, "I ask for forgiveness with all my asurean heart. I ask God to have mercy on me and I ask humanity to forgive everything I've done against it, for all the darkness I've levied upon it through the ages."

"And I repeat," said Carl, "that I forgive you on behalf of Man, with all my human heart, so help me God."

Yaldabaoth turned again to Carl, looking at him with a remorseful yet slightly hopeful countenance – an asurean and supernatural, yet repentant look. He thanked him in his innermost heart, Carl felt. Next, Hiranya gave the Dark Prince his hand. Yaldabaoth took it, again looking at Carl and nodding kindly, even smiling now 'the smile of the liberated'.

Carl nodded in return. This was a moment to remember. He then watched them all, Hiranya, Yaldabaoth and the heavenly host, venture off to the shore and be engulfed in an indescribable shimmer, ascending into the sky, it seemed, in a tunnel of light. In His Eighth Heaven, God watched all this and, as He always had done, He now again forgave Yaldabaoth.

Down on the Earth at the same time, a wave of light rushed forth and sent this new reality through people's hearts, a wave of light sent from God that was received by all devotees, by people who, in this moment, were induced to forgive even Yaldabaoth his wickedness. The new order came to happen everywhere as this golden light surged outwards and engulfed all of Sheol too, cleansing it, then continued down in a concentrated beam and instilled its goodness in The Land, first reaching the battlefield of Gnipaheden where the fighting was still continuing. By now the army of the Light had been encircled, the soldiers fighting with their backs to one another, surrounded on all sides by the howling hordes of the Dark. Piles of slain corpses lay in the middle of the enclosure as well as throughout Gnipaheden, both good and bad mixed together, united in deadly embraces.

But now the Light came from above and the white banner with the golden cross, set up in the middle of the encircled army, flew more boldly with the reality that flowed into it. Light and love joined in firm resolve to strengthen the emotions of the warriors' hearts and give them the renewed determination to go on the offensive again. The dark side, however, that hellish army with its demonic beliefs, its fighters cried out in pain as they felt this golden light cast over the plain. The flood of light from above spread across the battlefield like a shockwave, making them powerless, and like a storm wind the army of the Light attacked again in its wake. This divine wind hammered into the faces of the dark multitudes, defeating them with decisive combat; it ended the lives of the darkest warriors and scattered the rest, the few survivors fleeing into the neglected backwaters of the omniverse. Shaken but exultant, le Jeune and his captains knelt down and thanked God. The cloud cover lifted at once and the sun shone over Gnipaheden.

On the terrace of the dark glass beach house outside Sheol City, Carl and Ivan stood watching the heavenly host disappear and saw the divine light flow all around... and then everything disappeared, the beach house, Sheol, Ivan and all, and Carl felt as though he were falling through infinity. Everything became bright, so bright that everything went black.

CHAPTER TWENTY

BACK

A street and a church. A muddy street with wooden farmhouses and a whitewashed, eastern Catholic church at a junction of three roads. Carl sat in the saddle and looked around him, touching his forehead and gasping. 'What's happening, what am I doing here?' he thought. 'Wasn't I in Heaven just now, and didn't I redeem Yaldabaoth with my prayer?'

Clouds drifted by in the sky. For a moment everything swirled and swayed before him and Carl nearly fell from the saddle. 'Gather yourself, Captain!' he thought. 'You have a mission, to reconnoitre cantonments for the regimental staff. The goal was a certain castle, Castle Munte, wasn't it?' But first, he dismounted and went into the church to calm his mind. He rode up to the gate where he dismounted and tied up his horse before going inside; here there was light, colour and tranquility. He kept his gun belt and sword belt on because he was a soldier in a war and wouldn't let himself be surprised; however, he took off his service cap, entered the nave, went to a pew and sat down. Then he clasped his hands and calmed down, meditating on the nature of the inner light.

In a flash he remembered everything: Pelagion, the mission, Ivan and all their adventures together, The Rose That Never

Fades… and the road to Hell, sailing on a skull-and-bone ship, the meeting with Yaldabaoth and all that had happened afterwards. It was true, it had happened. Hadn't it?

Suddenly the church was filled by a bright light and appearing from it came Pelagion, the melancholy angel. He had the same tranquil countenance, the same silvery-grey lustre, the same blue-green frock with silver frontlet, and the same happy-sad aura as when he had first met him at the castle. Carl had to take a couple of deep breaths to steady himself.

"Pelagion," he said, standing up and bowing.

"Grey Knight," the angel greeted him and asked him to sit. Then he joined him in the pew. Carl paused for a moment, with many unanswered questions.

"What exactly is this world?" he began. "I mean, have I come to a different reality, one where I haven't been to Alexandru's castle yet? It's confusing. Am I back where I started, in the September of 1917 in a Romanian village, in Merlinatu?"

"Well," said the angel, "you are indeed here in Romania, back on Earth. But the important things you remember have indeed happened, it has all happened. You have drawn light to Yaldabaoth and freed the Devil from his darkness."

'Fine,' Carl thought with relief. 'Then everything didn't return to the primaeval state, to the Logos as Morven threatened.' In his heart of hearts, he had been a bit afraid of that. He may not be done with the everyday world yet but his mission had been completed and that felt fine.

"Yaldabaoth was won for the Light," the angel continued, "but in this world, the everyday world, your war is still going on because this world follows the laws of necessity. It's the implicit order of the material realm. Moreover, there are still residues of evil in the ether. Imprints of Yaldabaoth's evil thoughts remain here and there, and unfortunately these can be perceived by feeble minds, inspiring them to devilry."

"Well," Carl said, "you can't change everything, I suppose. But it all happened, you say, and I remember it and it feels good to have done what I've done. That said, there's still a question hanging over me, about my life now… If I was the intercessor, the good man in this story and the only one in the world who could pray for Yaldabaoth… well, what am I now? Do I continue to live on a perpetual moral plane, different to all others, with all the good things of life served up to me on a plate?"

"No, not at all," Pelagion said with a slight smile. "The goodness you have within you has to be rediscovered every day. It is the same for all good men and women, every day affirming and acknowledging the inner light anew. It must be done through meditation and by turning inwards, by bringing the mind to rest, quietening the inner monologue and focusing on things eternal instead of things material."

Carl nodded at this, realising how things stood. He recalled how he had fostered his will to resist the temptations of Morven on Gnipaheden, and realised that the same will is needed on a daily basis in order to live a decent life. We get nothing for free. We cannot take our grace for granted just because we once prayed a heartfelt prayer, however important that prayer might have been for the future of mankind, The Land and all of the omniverse. Then, as if coming to from a dream, he remembered something else.

"What has happened to Ivan?" he asked the angel, looking around with concern. "He was my great companion in the unknown worlds, in the mission to find the Rose and in Sheol."

"Ivan returned to The Land, the ethereal realm with its blazing campfires and shimmering castles, its green islands and fair maidens, the astral realm where everything is as you wish it to be."

"Aah," Carl nodded in understanding, "his place is in the land of adventure."

"Indeed. He had an urge to go back there, to be in The Land again and thus he has ended up there. When the wave of light flowed down from Heaven, Ivan began to think again about The Land with all its adventures and romantic ideas and he willed himself there – while you thought of this world, the Earth, the everyday world you came from. Therefore, you were brought here."

Pelagion rose and bowed slightly to the knight. Then the deva turned towards the shimmering light he had emerged from and Carl realised that he was leaving.

"So now we must part?"

"Yes, though we might meet again."

"Farewell, and thank you."

"Farewell, Grey Knight. You have made a difference. On behalf of Heaven, I thank you."

Pelagion disappeared in a ball of light. Carl breathed out, calmed down and his mind came to rest. Then he got up, put on his cap and walked out of the church. There he looked up into the blue sky seen between the clouds. And just then a horseman came riding down the street, mud flying from his steed's hooves in large clumps. The rider reined in and approached Carl where he stood.

"Captain Griffensteen?" he asked in Russian.

"The same."

"Ordered to reconnoitre cantonments for the regimental staff?"

Carl nodded.

"Counter-orders from the Colonel, sir. Return immediately, we're regrouping."

"In other words, we retreat?"

"It seems so."

Carl untied his own horse, mounted and returned to his unit accompanied by his new striker, riding through deserted villages, through dark forests and over meadows veiled in fire smoke, eventually reaching Alinescu. They crossed the park in the outskirts of town, took a shortcut through the ruins of buildings and entered the city proper, riding solemnly along the sandy streets. Having arrived at the HQ, Carl sought out the Colonel and reported to him about his abortive mission. Asked about Ivan, he simply said that his ADC had ridden astray.

Then a lot happened. The army retreated from the Romanian theatre of war, there was chaos and revolution in Russia, and Carl Griffensteen resigned from the Russian army with plans to return to his native land, Finland. The Bolsheviks took power in Russia in October, 1917 (by the Julian calendar). Carl, having been discharged, soon afterwards arrived in the capital, St Petersburg, by the Baltic Sea and bought a ticket for the next train home to Finland. The train would leave the following day, December 14, meaning an overnight stay at the Hotel Europe in the city centre; this was a venerable, luxury mansion with glazed wall tiles, mosaic floors and etched glass doors.

The city was now in the throes of the Bolshevik revolution, the socialist party of Lenin and Trotsky having taken political command of the Russian capital and a large part of the country in addition. After some years of civil war, they would command all of Russia.

As for Carl Griffensteen, he slept soundly in the hotel, the next morning heading for the Finlyandski railway station with a view to travelling home. By then, Finland had liberated itself from Russia, declaring itself an independent nation state. Although discharged, Carl still wore his army uniform since he owned these clothes and few others; an officer paid for his garb out of his own pocket. He wore greatcoat, grey tunic, cap, cavalry breeches and boots. The boots were as comfortable as ever, being the same pair he had worn during the rides throughout The Land and beyond. However, this day he didn't openly carry any weapons, his Nagant revolver being wrapped in a piece of cloth and carried in a bag.

Carl finally boarded his train and found his allotted compartment, a panelled closet with red plush seats. A man was already sitting there, a cavalry officer with a haughty expression. Having introduced himself, Carl learned that the man's name was Gustaf Mannerheim, like himself a former Russian army officer. The whistle blew and the train got moving, leaving the station and steaming off through the northern suburbs of St Petersburg in all their wintry splendour.

Mannerheim was a veritable myth-in-the-making, the future Commander-in-Chief in Finland's War of Liberation and in the Second World War. For now the pair continued talking about their respective Russian careers, the General describing a career similar to Carl's, a Finnish-Swedish nobleman born in Finland, conducting a military career in Tsarist Russia culminating in the First World War. Mannerheim, however, had had a longer run in it, being born in 1867 and having had his baptism of fire already in the Russo-Japanese War of 1904-05. After this he had had an adventurous ride through Asia, mainly in China. He mentioned a funny thing concerning that time: when issuing his passport, the Chinese official had asked him his name, eventually transcribing it as 'Ma–nu–ör–hei–mu'. Read in Chinese ideograms, this could be interpreted as 'The Horse that Rides over Clouds'.

"You're a true legend!" Carl exclaimed with a smile, hearing this. 'On the other hand,' Carl thought, 'I'm a legend in my own right too, maybe even more so than this Mannerheim fellow. Essentially I've done even more – I've fought the forces of true evil, prayed for the salvation of Yaldabaoth and saved mankind in the process, putting history on a more enlightened track.'

Riding in the comfortable compartment, while the wintery land of pine forest and snowy field passed by, lit by a pale sun, the General next discoursed on the current political situation, talking about the Red October Revolution in Russia which by this time had spread into Finland. Finland was formally free, having declared its independence from Russia in early December by forming a western-style democracy, but the situation was unstable with a Soviet-style rebellion brewing. Carl, usually not overly interested in politics, nonetheless listened attentively and decided to join the counter-revolutionary forces if civil war erupted.

To cut the story short, when Mannerheim arrived in Finland he was soon appointed Commander-in-Chief by the government in a process that led to the formation of the White Guards, a counter-revolutionary army in the service of the legal Finnish authorities. The formation of the army had to take place in Vasa on the west coast since Helsingfors, the capital, was taken over by the Red Guards in late January. Carl, for his part, had arrived in Helsingfors and seen the revolutionary chaos close at hand, so he had decided to leave the city in disguise and join the White Guards. Having reached Vasa, he reported for duty to Mannerheim himself and was given command of an infantry company, a function he served until joining Mannerheim in his triumphal homecoming to Helsingfors on the 15th of May, 1918. The civil war over, Finland could re-establish itself as a western democracy and the socialist menace was stopped at the eastern borders.

By now, Carl had had his fill of combat, having been in the line of fire since 1914. He took his leave, re-established himself in Helsingfors and got a job as a personnel manager at the Dickursby paint company. Life was quite good except for the inevitable post-war hardships; but it was peace, Finland was free and Carl had a job to go to. He also had a mistress and a circle of friends, and he settled well into civilian life considering having been a front-line soldier for a long time. He started to enjoy the peacetime life, in the ordinary world of 1920s Finland.

Sometimes he would remember his adventures in Romania and beyond, in the dreamy vistas of The Land. Had it all really happened? He often asked himself this. Moreover, if he had in fact redeemed the Devil, then why was the world still a noisy confusion of strife, needs and problems? Well, that depended on man's free will, he had to tell himself. He, Carl, might have drawn light into Sheol and Yaldabaoth, paving the way for a brighter future for mankind, but mankind as a whole also had to choose light rather than darkness. It could never be enough for one man to have chosen it, by praying for the redemption of Yaldabaoth. And so the world continued on its course without becoming a shining paradise, without Heaven being manifested on Earth; Morven, for his part, had intimated such a thing to Carl before the Gnipaheden battle.

Carl didn't actually remember that. His mind focused on the question of whether his adventures had been real. They had, Pelagion had told him so when they had met in the Merlinatu church after his return to the everyday world. But Carl seemed to have forgotten this too.

One day, however, Carl stumbled into Pelagion again, who proved that it hadn't been a dream.

CHAPTER TWENTY-ONE
GREENSLEEVES

It was on a Helsingfors avenue, one day in August 1922, that Carl chanced upon Pelagion, the angel who had first urged him to go to The Land and set out on the quest for The Rose That Never Fades, with all that followed.

Pelagion still wore his hair long, however he wasn't clad in robes now, instead sporting a topcoat and a Homburger hat. Nonetheless, Carl immediately recognised the figure's countenance, the other-worldly features with their tinge of melancholy. The long hair looked rather incongruous under the hat and alongside clothes that signalled formality and 'a pillar of society', making the angel look like a sort of 1920s artistic type. But there were many odd people around in those times and Pelagion wasn't so much distinctive from the city people of Helsingfors at that time. In cities, one meets all kinds of people, even a long-haired angel of God in a Homburger hat.

"It's really good to meet you again," Carl said when the first surprise had abated.

"Nice to meet you, too," the angel said. "I had a premonition that you may need a visit from me. So here I am."

Indeed, Carl still had some questions he wanted answers for. They walked alongside a park with green maples, magpies cawing above and a mild wind blowing, this overcast day that had earlier seen some rain. Heading for a café, Carl asked bluntly whether The Land had been real and whether his actions there had actually taken place.

"Yes, they did," the deva confirmed, patiently. "And you did meet me in this world, in Castle Munte and in The Land also. The battle at Gnipaheden did take place."

Once at the café they entered and took off their coats and hats, found a table and ordered coffees, Carl having a Napoleon pastry to go with his while Pelagion was satisfied without eating. They admired the interior of chequered floor, teak chairs and sofas with leather seats and walls decorated with landscape paintings. Carl tasted his pastry, wiping the traces of whipped cream and red confectioner's sugar from the corners of his mouth before producing his pipe and stuffing it with *Gävle Vapen*, as was his habit in this life as well as in the astral worlds.

Blowing out the cool smoke, Carl started talking about the existence of evil. Yes, he already knew that the world was still a messy place and evil hadn't been uprooted in spite of the redemption of Yaldabaoth and the cleansing of Sheol. But what was Pelagion's view on it all? What had Carl's prayer for Yaldabaoth actually resulted in?

"Well," the angel said, "indeed you were there at Gnipaheden and in Sheol too, and you met Yaldabaoth and all that. But Man still has free will so he can go on doing as he wishes. This is the nature of being human. And as I said to you in Merlinatu, there are still traces of evil in the ether, the invisible, soulful atmosphere – these residues tend to attract the more materialistic people. People without a strong will and ethic tend to become ruled by their needs and desires, and blindly going after one's needs and desires can make one evil. Therefore evil still exists.

"But your intercession did indeed have an effect on the future existence of Man, on the esoteric climate as a whole. Darkness may again try to gain the upper hand but it'll be harder now that Yaldabaoth has turned to the Light."

Having said this, Pelagion looked wistfully out over the park beyond the window while Carl for his part put the pipe aside and finished his pastry. He smiled at the memory of his Sheol adventure and then began to wonder about the fate of Yaldabaoth, asking what had become of him after the heavenly host had come down to meet the prodigal one.

"Yaldabaoth was taken to the Eighth Heaven where he met his spiritual Father," Pelagion replied. "It was a touching scene. All was peace. A vibration of joy and love permeated Heaven in that moment, yes, all the Heavens and all of the Earth, The Land and the entire omniverse. A renewed emanation of light and love started to play the basic chord of existence and angels sang for their long-lost brother as he came home.

"Yaldabaoth was then taken to a certain astral dwelling with flowerbeds, fountains and temples where he was given a home to rest in, assisted by angels and devas. His asurean children also came to visit him, those who had also repented earlier and asked to be forgiven. Even his once partner, Athena Pronoia, was there. It was all very touching."

Going for a refill and returning with steaming cups, Carl sat down again and asked for more information about heavenly matters. He pressed Pelagion to tell him more about creation, the true story of it, filling in the gaps of the sometimes sketchy narrative of the Bible, which was all Carl had known. Pelagion patiently gave the necessary facts and pointed out that the Bible wasn't entirely wrong about such things, it just tended to express esoteric matters in symbolic form.

There were many more questions in Carl's mind for the deva, such as whether he would ever meet his soulmate in this life, the Greensleeves woman whom he had encountered in life after life according to the Book of Life. But he knew that it was useless to ask this. Not even angels can be expected to know everything about everyone. Maybe he would meet her, maybe not. Was it still written in the stars? But then, every man has freedom to create and shape his own life.

This thought led Carl to a humorous idea, as he sat in that Helsingfors café with the angel. Perhaps he could place an advertisement in the newspapers, saying, "LOST! Your soul name is Greensleeves. We last met in the 19th century. living in the Biedermeier era, with me dying just before La Belle Epoque. You were my sister and I was your brother. You had green eyes and a lovely smile. Answer to Silverstar."

Carl continued with his everyday life in 1920s Finland, changing careers from paint company official to teacher of Russian, a language he knew well. Then, in the mid-1930s, his elder brother Axel died childless and Carl inherited the family estate. As head of the family, becoming the new Baron Griffensteen, he now took on the responsibilities that came with this, such as maintaining the manor, leasing out farmland, selling timber and speaking at community celebrations. And he did everything else that a landed lord does, including riding his horse along the roads and the woodland paths.

He remained a bachelor, enjoying reading his spiritual books and eventually acquiring some 'talent for living' – the ability to find joy in small things and accepting that this is one's life, the best life. As time passed in the country, Carl sometimes remembered a special aspect of his adventures in The Land, his reading in the Book of Life and learning of his successive reincarnations with the Silverstar and Greensleeves narrative.

Greensleeves, that alluring name, that haunting image. He missed his true, eternal companion in all these lives, his green-eyed woman. He had met her from the Stone Age through ancient, mediaeval and modern times, whether as sister or wife, as friend or lover. She had always been there, in every life. Except this one…

One overcast summer day in 1936, a car came up the long drive-way and halted in the yard. It was a maroon red Volvo, the type with much sheet metal in the bodywork, the `35 model. A woman stepped out of the vehicle, approached and knocked at the manager's wing to ask for directions. It happened to be Carl who opened the door. But quite what she said about where she was going he didn't even hear, for he found himself looking directly into that pair of lovely green eyes. He melted away on the spot, unable to speak; she also then seemed lost for words, recognising her own Silverstar unconsciously.

"Won't you come in and… sit down?"

She accepted, this slim, blonde apparition with freckles and unmistakeable charm. She was led into the kitchen where Carl took her coat and put it absentmindedly on a chair, put the coffee on and felt at peace. He was totally at peace, for he knew then and there that this was She, while she also knew that it was He. But neither of them said it aloud.

Her name was Harriet Sundqvist and she was from Vasa, work-ing as a teacher. She was thirty years old. Currently, she was simply out driving in the neighbourhood since teachers' holidays are long.

"Grey weather today," Carl observed, for something to say, and looked out over the yard, over the trees and the sky. Harriet nodded.

"Mmm, it's a bit grey. What a summer, huh?"

"But it's only the third of July yet. In the middle of the month it's always hot."

"Really?"

"Indeed. Dog Days, you know."

"Um…?"

"That's when things rot. Food can't be left out of the 'fridge too long and so on."

This banal conversation took place without it mattering one bit to the universe or to history and all. But it was important to Carl. It was as though he had always lived with her. He felt that they could have been living together for twenty years of marriage, or fifty or whatever. The tone of voice, the way to listen, everything in their conversation was easy and to the point.

They had found one another.

The coffee was ready. They drank it and looked at each other and said nothing, the silence being enough.

Then Carl spotted something: Harriet wore a ring on her hand, a golden jade ring with an engraved bird. He remembered it! As the mediaeval knight Guillaume he had, as told in the Book of Life, once escorted a nun to a convent. She was named Laureline. They had conversed deeply during that journey and she had worn exactly this ring, he was sure of it.

"Let me see your ring, please," he said.

Harriet held out her hand. He already knew that this was the same ring and that Harriet had been Laureline in that previous life, just as he had been Guillaume, there in 1300s France. However, Harriet was yet unaware of her previous lives.

"Where did you get the ring?" he asked, seemingly unmoved.

"This one?" said Harriet. "My Dad bought it in France once. I got it when I was confirmed."

"Where?"

"What?"

"Where did he get it?"

"Oh, in an antique shop. Why?"

"No, it's nothing."

Laureline's ring had lived its own life since given to Guillaume and then, on his deathbed, having been taken off his finger by his wife and put away in a box. From this obscure place, the treasure had eventually ended up in an antique shop. And here it was now, on a strange yet familiar woman's finger. Carl said nothing more about it. But now he was sure that Harriet was the reincarnated Greensleeves. By some magical, karmic force the ring had returned to the possession of the woman who, in a previous life, had owned it.

Harriet asked about the farming business and he told her all about it with boyish joy. 'I'm happy again,' he thought. 'I've had a good life but it's been a long time since I laughed. However, with her I can smile.'

A maid came and cooked dinner for two, Carl and Harriet, then the maid left. Harriet was invited to sleep over, in a private room of course, and she accepted the invitation.

They married after six months, in Åbo church, in January, 1937. The honeymoon was spent on Easter Island in the Pacific Ocean, then they both settled down on the estate. Harriet got a teaching position in the district, in Rotenbo village school.

They loved one another, Harriet and Carl. It was a perfect match and they just belonged together as soulmates do. It was a relationship guided by a natural feeling, with no need for courtship or anxiety; they knew where they were with one another. Theirs was a match made in Heaven. Carl, however, was silent about his knowledge of their particular astral kinship, their successive incarnations together. He was afraid that talking about it might sabotage the whole thing. It was Harriet, however, who brought it up on a warm midsummer's evening in 1937, in the bedroom of the manager's wing. Lying in bed with her husband, Harriet became thoughtful.

"I can't get rid of this feeling."

"What's that?"

"That we've met before."

Carl now had a moment of soul-searching. Could he just say, 'Yes, we met aeons ago in the astral world as twin flames, as a primordial man and woman, as a *dyad*, each other's dual.' He was afraid that Harriet would baulk at the occult perspective and that this would create a rift in their relationship, even destroy it completely.

But then he thought, 'Am I, the Grey Knight, having faced the Devil, the army of the Dark and Morven, now in 1937 afraid of being abandoned by the woman I love, simply because of revealing the esoteric truth to her?' Indeed, it was a moment of truth so he thought, 'Now or never.'

"Darling," he said, "we have indeed met before, in previous lives."

"How do you mean, 'previous lives'?"

"Since the dawn of time, we have lived together, you and I."

So he told her of their lives as Greensleeves and Silverstar from the Stone Age to the present, of their intimacy as lovers, as husband and wife, siblings and relatives or just as friends. Throughout ancient, mediaeval and modern times, they had met and separated again and again. But no meeting was the first and no farewell was the last. Harriet listened attentively, her expression changing from surprised and shocked to charmed and then spiritually enlightened.

"Greensleeves," she eventually said with delight. "I am Greensleeves."

"And I am Silverstar," Carl said. "We're a soul pair, twin flames, together forever and until the end of time."

Harriet then reached out for her bedside table, picked up a ring lying on it and showed it to Carl. "It's the ring, the jade ring. The one I carried in my earlier life as Laureline, the mediaeval French nun."

"Indeed it is," Carl said, admiring the engraved jade bird. "The ring that I, as Guillaume, received as a gift from you before you died."

"And eventually it was found by my father and given to me. And you saw it when I wore it at our first meeting."

"Our first meeting in *this* life. No meeting is the first and no farewell is the last."

"Indeed, I see that now," Harriet said, putting her hand on Carl's shoulder. "My eternal man," she added.

"And you are my eternal woman."

Beyond the window, the branches of a maple tree waved in the night breeze. Ragged clouds drifted past a moon shining down onto the bed where the pair now slept soundly in each other's arms, Carl and Harriet, the Grey Knight and his wife, Silverstar and Greensleeves.

If you have enjoyed this book...

Local Legend is committed to publishing the very best spiritual writing, both fiction and non-fiction. You might also enjoy:

PATHWAYS OF THE DRUIDS

Christopher J Pine (ISBN 978-1-907203-61-9)

Christopher J Pine's wonderful debut novel is an exciting blend of fantasy, myth, magic and history. A real page-turning adventure story for all ages. In AD 60, the Roman Empire occupies Britannia and the ancient culture and freedoms of the Celts are being destroyed. Guided by the Druid priests, Boudicca leads the Iceni in an uprising against Nero's forces. It's a losing battle. However, the Druids have a mastery of nature, and skills far beyond those of the Romans. They devise a final desperate strategy to avoid slavery, and summon their greatest magic yet to open a portal into the alternative world of Triannaib. One last Celtic tribe, the Ordoveteii, race to cross the threshold...

DAY TRIPS TO HEAVEN

T J Hobbs (ISBN 978-1-907203-99-2)

The author's debut novel is a brilliant description of life in the spiritual worlds and of the guidance available to all of us on Earth as we struggle to be the best we can. Ethan is learning to be a guide but having a hard time of it, with too many questions and too much self-doubt. But he has potential, so is given a special dispensation to bring a few deserving souls for a preview of the afterlife, to help them with crucial decisions they have to make in their lives. The book is full of gentle humour, compassion and spiritual knowledge, and it asks important questions of us all.

AURA CHILD

A I Kaymen (ISBN 978-1-907203-71-8)

One of the most astonishing books ever written, telling the true story of a genuine Indigo child. Genevieve grew up in a normal London family but from an early age realised that she had very special spiritual and psychic gifts. She saw the energy fields around living things, read people's thoughts and even found herself slipping through time, able to converse with the spirits of those who had lived in her neighbourhood. This is an uplifting and inspiring book for what it tells us about the nature of our minds.

A SINGLE PETAL

Oliver Eade (ISBN 978-1-907203-42-8)

Winner of the national Local Legend Spiritual Writing Competition, this page-turner is a novel of murder, politics and passion set in ancient China. Yet its themes of loyalty, commitment and deep personal love are every bit as relevant for us today as they were in past times. The author is an expert on Chinese culture and history, and his debut adult novel deserves to become a classic.

A UNIVERSAL GUIDE TO HAPPINESS

Joanne Gregory (ISBN 978-1-910027-06-6)

Joanne is an internationally acclaimed clairaudient medium with a celebrity contact list. Growing up, she ignored her evident psychic abilities, fearful of standing out from others, and even later, despite witnessing miracles daily, her life was difficult. But then she began to learn the difference between the psychic and the spiritual, and her life turned round. This is her spiritual reference handbook, a guide to living happily and successfully in harmony with the energy that created our universe. It is the knowledge and wisdom distilled from a lifetime's experience of working with spirit.

THE QUIRKY MEDIUM

Alison Wynne-Ryder (ISBN 978-1-907203-47-3)

Alison is the co-host of the TV show *Rescue Mediums*, in which she puts herself in real danger to free homes of lost and often malicious spirits. Yet she is a most reluctant medium, afraid of ghosts! This is her amazing and often very funny autobiography, taking us 'backstage' of the television production as well as describing how she came to discover the psychic gifts that have brought her an international following.

Winner of the Silver Medal in the national Wishing Shelf Book Awards.

5P1R1T R3V3L4T10N5

Nigel Peace (ISBN 978-1-907203-14-5)

With descriptions of more than a hundred proven prophetic dreams and many more everyday synchronicities, the author shows us that, without doubt, we can know the future and that everyone can receive genuine spiritual guidance for our lives' challenges. World-renowned biologist Dr Rupert Sheldrake has endorsed this book as "...vivid and fascinating... pioneering research..." and it was national runner-up in The People's Book Prize awards.

These titles are all available as paperbacks and eBooks.
Further details and extracts of these and many
other beautiful books may be seen at

www.local-legend.co.uk

www.ingramcontent.com/pod-product-compliance
Lightning Source LLC
Chambersburg PA
CBHW061324200626
46813CB00017B/2859